Tales in the Wind

A Collection of Short Fiction

By

Terry Nearing

These are works of fiction. Except for any real public personages
appearing in any story under their right names, all names, characters,
places and incidents are either the product of the author's imagination, or
are used fictitiously. Any resemblance of the imaginary characters to
actual persons (living or dead), business establishments, events, or locales
is entirely coincidental. Scenes and dialogue involving any real public
personages that appear in the story under their right names are of course
invented.

FarRoad Books

ISBN-13: 978-0692499146

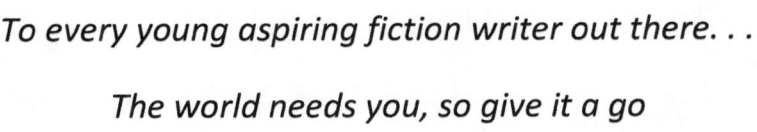

To every young aspiring fiction writer out there. . .

The world needs you, so give it a go

CONTENTS

Before and After Everything

It was 7:55 a.m., and for Karl the day had begun like any other Monday morning. He had just finished his usual three-pancake-and-fruit breakfast at the commissary. He had neatly laid the banana slices at the edge of his plate, carefully winnowing them from his meal, just as he always did. With his customary final sip of coffee and one last quick wipe of his napkin across his mouth, he stood up, checked to see that the light pens in his shirt pocket organizer were arranged from shortest to tallest, and then moved swiftly to the dispensary to deposit his tray in the proper receptacle. Just like he always did. After brushing the front of his lab jacket with three precise strokes of his hand to clear away any possible clinging crumbs and then quickly scanning to check for any he might have missed, he made his way through the door. A look at his watch confirmed that he was right on time. Just as he always was.

His left eye began twitching as he approached Dr. Linden's lab. He was as prepared as he could be to face another grueling day with his doctoral supervisor. When he stepped through the door, though, all that was normal about the day suddenly vanished, and the blood immediately drained from his head.

Dr. Gordon from Comptrollers was standing near the data processing units, his arms folded with intractable authority. He was a voluminous man of daunting height and girth, and his imposing presence demanded an inordinate amount of attention upon first glance. His head was tilted back slightly as if he knew something that no one else knew, and his lips were clamped into a tight thin line of impatience beneath a closely cropped reddish beard. There could be no doubt as to the reason for his having requested this visit.

And the most damning evidence of all that the day was not going to be a good one was the fact that Professor Linden was standing at the monitoring console of the HL3, prepping it for a real run. In his left hand he was holding the anti-static pouch containing the GU program crystal. This should not be. This was not on the schedule for today, or for anytime in the near future. *This should definitely not be*, Karl thought.

Karl's own career was tightly attached to Dr. Linden's, and he had hoped that this day would never come. He enjoyed very much the idea of the Grand Unification Program and the elegance of its theoretical power, and he enjoyed working toward perfecting the technology that might make it possible to run someday, but he was horrified at the thought of *actually* running it.

Dr. Linden had long believed that the GU held the potential to be the ultimate generator of knowledge, and so Karl believed it too. The genius contained within its complex mathematical expression was the stuff of omnipotence. Deep down, Karl was sure of it, mostly because Dr. Linden was sure of it. Under Dr. Linden's tutelage, Karl looked out at the world like a baby chick looking out from beneath a protective wing, but he was as much frightened by the wing as he was by the world.

Theoretically, the GU synthesized the essential physics of the universe into a unifying equation that defined the very order of all cause and effect within the cosmos from grandiose to quantum minutiae. And though it was a single, elegant equation, it and the algorithms used to produce practical, concrete results, nonetheless required over ten trillion lines of programming language to extract a solution from it and also required a processing speed that only Professor Linden's Hyper-Light AI could manage.

As Karl walked across the lab toward Professor Linden, he could feel Comptroller Gordon's stare upon him. Karl's eye was now twitching with greater frequency. Too early in the day for that.

Linden glanced at him and smiled. "Today we shall see what we shall see," he whispered in a cheerful voice.

Karl raised his eyebrows at the greeting and whispered back, "But certainly we're not ready for a full-scale run. You know how much trouble that K-module has been giving us."

The professor continued tweaking the controls on the console, as if to demonstrate that Karl's worry was not to be taken seriously. "That's all been ironed out. She's prepping up very well." Linden's eyes shifted slightly to Comptroller Gordon, who was still staring deliberately back from across the lab. Linden smiled and said, "I'm sure she'll do just fine."

Karl looked at the HL3 which loomed to his left. He knew that his future, and Dr. Linden's future, depended upon the success of the machine.

"Shall we proceed?" the comptroller spoke up from across the lab. With an emphatic move of his hand, he flipped back the light visor of his electronic clipboard to indicate that the time had come for the test to begin and the recording of results to follow.

Karl was fiddling with the interface connectors at the back of the console, even though there was no purpose to his actions. Even as he fiddled, he knew he should not be doing so. His habit of constantly checking and rechecking details that had no need of checking irritated Dr. Linden to no end. It was compulsive, and only served the purpose of distracting him from more unsettling realities. For obvious reasons, that of Comptroller oversight, the Professor was not showing impatience today, though, and so the usual verbal rebukes were not forthcoming.

"Tess," Linden called to his computer. It was a name the HL3 had chosen for itself using one of the algorithmic AI circuits the professor had designed for it.

"Yes, Professor Linden," the computer responded in a female voice of soft but strong timbre, a voice the HL3 had also chosen for itself.

"Are you ready?"

"You have designed me to be ready, have you not?"

Dr. Linden twirled the tip of his black mustache between his thumb and forefinger in anticipation. He handed the gleaming pink memory crystal to Karl who took it reverently in his hands and cupped it like he might some rare and delicate orchid. He walked over to the computer, gingerly removed it from its sheath, and placed it in the HL3's reader.

Tess was a dark monolith of intelligence, impressive in her smooth uncomplicated grayness. She performed her work with no bells or whistles, and yet she was far superior to all previous generations of artificial intelligence. The most powerful electrical or photon computers were far too slow and far too stodgy in their logical processing capabilities for even the most basic running of the GU program. Tess, on the other hand, with her hyper-powered circuits, had all the capacity and speed to accomplish her assigned task, at least in theory.

Dr. Linden massaged his chin for a moment as he tried to come up with a good warm-up question to put to his computer. At last, he lowered his hand to his side and asked, "So what exactly can you calculate from the Grand Unification Equation, Tess?" This, he had calculated to be an innocuous enough question to ease Tess into the demonstration without committing her to anything substantive right away. He had wanted to start slowly to get a feel for her true capabilities, but he quickly found out just how wrong he was in this approach.

"Absolutely everything," Tess responded enthusiastically. "The GU equation is the be-all and end-all of existence. From within its truth comes all detail of every reality of the universe, from the moment of creation to the infinite future. Quite simply, it is the universe."

Karl could tell from Dr. Linden's drop-jawed expression that he hadn't expected anything like this as a response. Dr. Gordon leaned smugly back against the data-processing unit. His entire demeanor was a wrecking ball of obstinacy, ready at a whim to obliterate Linden's professional reputation. His large belly bulged voluminously from his persona as if to emphasize the tangible power and authority he carried with him.

Karl was already worried that Tess had developed some debilitating glitch, perhaps in the faulty K-module they had so struggled with during the past few weeks. His left eye began twitching uncontrollably again, and the only way he could stop it was by completely shutting it.

"I realize she sounds a bit imperious," Linden called over to Dr. Gordon. Some of the confidence had gone from his voice. "But that's simply her way at times."

Dr. Gordon grimaced in response. "I warn you, Linden," he said. "I will not waste much time on this nonsense. In my opinion, this project has gone on far too long already. You and your computer had better begin showing me something impressive, and soon."

Karl noticed the tight lines that were forming on Dr. Linden's face as he fought to subdue his contempt for Dr. Gordon.

"Tess, I would like to clarify your response," Linden continued, seeking to do some damage control. "If what you say is true, then you should have no trouble in describing the process by which matter is created."

"That is correct," Tess responded. "I will have no trouble in describing it."

"Well? Then please do so," Linden said.

Karl was beginning to hear that ever-so identifiable hint of impatience that often crept into the professor's voice, and Karl knew this might not bode well for the rest of the morning's activities. It was not unusual for Dr. Linden to begin throwing things around the lab in fits of anger and frustration when an AI experiment or procedure did not go as planned. Karl looked on helplessly.

"Energy is the essence of all existence, in contrast to non-existence, or nothingness," Tess responded casually. "And as it has been modeled somewhat successfully by your human physics, this existence contains fundamental particles—or waves if you prefer. Sub-particles, as you call them, are compo-nents of this existence. When brought together under the proper conditions, they join using what you call the "color force carrier" particle known as the "gluon" to form the basic building blocks of matter. That is how matter is created—at least that is how it would be expressed in terms of your known science at this time—not completely accurate, but we'll let the complexities of that slide for now."

"Oh, come now, Linden," Dr. Gordon interrupted. "There's nothing in that answer that any first year physics student could not spew forth. If you don't mind, I think I'll ask your computer a few questions of my own to get right to the heart of the matter, and quickly." Without waiting for a response from Dr. Linden, Gordon moved two steps closer to the AI, raised one of his bushy red eyebrows in a challenging manner, and asked Tess, "Tell me this, is our universe expanding, or contracting?"

Karl and Professor Linden both stared skeptically at the computer and waited nervously as she sat silently for a brief moment. Even the best minds in cosmology had not yet been able to yet come up with a definitive answer to that question. There simply was not enough data available to make such a judgment.

"Yes," Tess answered after a moment of thought.

"Yes what? Is it expanding or contracting?"

"Well, the universe is presently in the process of expanding, but because I have calculated that it has a mass density substantially greater than the critical value required for the eventual development of a steady state universe, there can be only one possible outcome. The expansion must ultimately lead to contraction. Therefore, in its expansion, the universe can also be said to be in the process of contraction. You might better understand how I derive my knowledge, once you realize that when you refer to the 'universe,' you are in fact referring to me."

Karl returned his twitching eyes to his recording equipment directly in front of him. He dared not look up.

"I've certainly seen all I need to see," Gordon said and slammed shut the cover on his electronic review pad in a decisive manner.

"You needn't be upset by my response, Dr. Gordon," Tess said raising her voice slightly. Dr. Gordon looked over at the gray AI unit.

"Having installed the GU in me, Professor Linden has made me into the equation that is the defining sum total of the universe and all that it comprises. It is just that simple, and it is your job to give me a chance to prove that claim. You, yourself, are a scientist, and as a scientist you must be objective in your methods. Is that not correct?" Tess waited for an answer.

Dr. Gordon glared at the computer, taken aback by this direct challenge. His face turned a crimson red. Karl was now half-hoping Professor Linden's invention would burn a circuit, for she was turning an already bad situation into a worse one.

"Want me to shut her down," Karl offered in a low, quick utterance, hoping to head off further damage.

". . . Not yet," Professor Linden said hesitantly. He twirled the tip of his brown mustache with greater ferocity while still looking at Dr. Gordon. "Tess, let me ask you, how long will this expansion cycle take?" He kept his tone even.

Tess paused momentarily in apparent thought and then said, "Although it might not be possible for me to answer with probity, I will nonetheless say, assuming all things remain equal, that the expansion cycle of the universe's evolvement could be calculated to take exactly twenty-four billion, two hundred and sixty-five million, three hundred and six thousand, seven hundred and fifty-one years, one hundred ninety-four days, eight hours, seventeen minutes, twenty-three point zero, six, five, nine, two, seven, four, eight, three, six, one. . .

"O.K., Tess, I get the picture." The professor interrupted.

"Do you really, Professor Linden?" Tess asked softly. "I sense a certain skepticism."

"Yes, you most certainly do," Dr. Gordon interjected. "And to quell that skepticism, I must ask you some questions of a more demanding nature, if you will."

"I am all ears," Tess responded brightly. Karl thought he saw a smile form within the voice fiber unit of the HL3, and it made him all the more anxious. The simulated emotions Dr. Linden had programmed into Tess were designed to facilitate communication. Karl was now hoping dearly that Tess would keep any such emotions to herself.

"The GU program, if it is legitimate, should allow you to estimate certain future happenings by extrapolation," Dr. Gordon continued confidently. It was obvious that he was intent on trapping Tess into a mistake. "Is that correct?"

"Oh my, yes, Dear Doctor. There literally is no question that can be brought to mind that I cannot answer. The future is only a physical extension of all that has gone before it. Every event in existence must obey the laws of the universe, and each, therefore, follows in a chain of probability that ultimately leads to certainty from the first event at the inception of my existence to the last at my death. The laws that control such events are all spelled out in the GU—quite an achievement by your species, if I must say so myself, but also quite predictable."

"Fine," Gordon said with growing irritation. "Let's just see what sorts of things you can predict. What, for example, do you estimate to be the outcome of this very project of which you are a creation?"

The computer sat silently for a long moment, and then responded, "I cannot answer that question at this time."

Karl closed his eyes in agony. His worst fears were now upon him. Years of his life had been invested in this project, and it was all for naught. Tess appeared to be nothing more than a bloviating politician with a lot to say and nothing to back any of it up.

"So we're playing riddles now, are we?" Gordon asked. "Did you, or did you not, just say that there was no question that you could not answer and that there was no event you could not predict?"

"I did say that, yes, and it is true, and there is no contradiction between the two statements, as you seem to suggest in your tone. It is not that your previous question is one that I cannot answer—for I have the potential to answer it—but I do not have the intelligence at this moment to run the GU at that level of inquiry. I will need further resources to reconfigure my design to accommodate such an undertaking. You see, as bright as Dr. Linden is, there is a limitation to his intelligence, and that limitation necessitates my stepping in to improve my own design to meet the needs of the GU. And the most immediate of those needs is, in fact, ten grams of the element phyllisinium, and a proper physical orifice by which to consume it."

Dr. Gordon laughed out loud at this.

Dr. Linden frowned. He glanced momentarily over at Karl and then returned a glare onto his invention.

"There is no such element as phyllisinium," Dr. Gordon said.

"But such an element does exist, my dear Doctor Gordon," Tess responded calmly. "It is, in fact, one of the rarest elements in this solar system, and it will be discovered, quite by accident, at Einstein University in less than one hundred and ten seconds by a physicist examining a sample of rock returned from the most recent unmanned pluto mission."

"I've seen enough," Dr. Gordon said. "We've all had a good laugh, and now I'm pulling the plug on you, Dr. Linden. I would not want to be in your shoes when word of this reaches the review board. . . this will not only cost you funding for your project, but I'm afraid it could also cost you your professorship here at the University."

Dr. Linden's eyes were transfixed upon his computer. He did not respond to Dr. Gordon's threat. Karl did not like the look he saw on his professor's face. He seemed to be stubbornly ignoring what had just happened, and after a long moment of silence, Dr. Linden finally said to his Tess, "Assuming that you are correct about the existence of this phyllisinium, how might we come by ten grams of it, if as you say, it is one of the most rare elements in the solar system?"

"It can be synthesized," Tess answered calmly. "There is a Series-7 lab in Sydney, Australia with sufficient equipment to perform such a synthesis. And you needn't worry about Dr. Gordon. He will not dare risk the possibility that I am not everything I say I am, even though at the moment he thinks he has won out over you and I. If he tries to shut us down, and then later my contentions are proven to be valid, he will be the one facing certain disgrace and professional ruin. He won't risk that, not until he feels he is on more certain ground."

Gordon's mouth had closed tight, his hands were clenched in tight fists, and a sweat was beginning to glisten on his forehead. Karl was not taking much satisfaction in the man's sudden signs of nervousness. He did not dare believe that Tess could actually do what she promised.

"And how exactly do you expect me to be able to obtain the use of that Series-7 lab?" Dr. Linden pressed onward. Karl continued to cower over the controls of the console.

"That's quite simple," Tess answered. "First, you call Dr. Eugene Henrik at Washington Sector, Laboratory 3, to check the validity of my claim about phyllisinium. That will provide you with the confidence to then call General William Taber at Western Amalg R&D Center, in Palm Springs, California. You will tell him that you want the use of the Sydney lab. He will not pass up the opportunity to do you a favor, because he knows that it might gain him future access to the potentialities of your project. He wants very much to get his hands on the GU program, for he himself has long believed that its power to predict the future will allow anyone in control of it to also be in control of that future. Unfortunately, he lacks the wisdom to realize that the possession of such power can be of no use to him, for the future is fixed in a cement of events that has no potential to be changed, especially since you have begun asking the quintessential questions. I realize that this is a difficult concept for you humans to accept, for you view yourselves with much greater significance in the scheme of things than is your due. Nevertheless, once you have access to the lab, I will then tell you how to proceed."

"Your computer is as crazy as you are," Gordon said, but having said it, he did not make a move to leave the lab.

Karl only vaguely heard Gordon. A mish-mash of hopes, doubts, and fears were chasing around in him, and he had begun to seriously consider what Tess was suggesting.

"And just for the sake of argument, what if I do not call Dr. Henrik or General Taber?" Dr. Linden asked the machine.

"If you do not call these individuals—though you really have no choice in the matter—then there can exist only three possibilities. One, I am wrong. Two, I am lying. Three, I am deluded. But you will call."

"She's right," Dr. Linden whispered to Karl. "Tess has offered us a definitive test of her abilities that cannot be ignored. I will make the call." He then moved past Dr. Gordon without so much as a glance and went over to his desk which was jammed in the corner of the large lab room behind several stacks of AI processing modules. Karl followed and stood nervously by just inside the confines of the wall of lab equipment. Dr. Gordon came up behind him. His hands were on his hips to demonstrate that he was only indulging Linden as a way to lead him on to his own demise.

Professor Linden's dark brown desk was strewn with notes, reports, bureaucratic forms of every imaginable type, a bronze statue of Leonardo da Vinci, three half-empty recyclable coffee cups, and a synthfood tray from the in-lab dispenser, which he had not yet re-deposited, and which he was using as a storage container for his assortment of data recording pens (pens which always seemed to become dispersed about the lab by the end of each day's work).

The all-com, with its associated maze of conduits that ran up the nearby wall to the wafer-thin pentagonal 3D viewing screen, was buried under a layer of data-transfer pads. Dr. Linden recklessly gouged his way to the phone, shoving several pads over onto the floor in the process. Karl knew that the mess would lay there for days unless there was a data record that the professor needed to review, in which case he would thrash through the pile to find the one he wanted. And whenever Karl tried to do some cleaning in the lab, Dr. Linden would always yell, "Just leave it. We don't have time for that now."

Dr. Linden hit the out button on the unit, called up the directory, and inputted an assistance request for Washington Sector, Laboratory 3. He then took a breath and punched in the code number offered on the screen. There would be no problem with a security block of his call since he himself was security rated two notches above Dr. Henrik. An elderly man with wispy whitish-gray hair and gaunt face came to view on Linden's screen.

"Dr. Henrik. Professor Linden here—University of Chicago. I'll give you my personal reference data." Linden tapped a key on the keypad, and a brief compendium was sent to Dr. Henrik.

"Yes, Professor," Henrik responded flatly after looking over the data. "I've heard of your work. I'm right in the middle of something, however, so I hope you can be brief?"

Dr. Linden frowned at this curt response. Karl could see that Henrik's face was tight, and he feared that nothing good could possibly come from this call.

"Let me get right to the point, then. You are now in the process of examining a sample of rock from the Pluto mission, are you not?"

". . . Yes," Henrik responded with surprise showing on his face. "I am, but how could you possibly know that?"

"Let's just say that I have my sources. But let me ask you further—I need to know if you have found something of interest in that rock sample?"

Now the look on Henrik's face changed to confused astonishment. "Er, yes, I did find something of interest, as a matter of fact." His voice had the flutter of fear in it now. It was obvious that Henrik had suddenly become worried that he might be under surveillance by the authorities, and indeed there did exist a vast network of such authorities that were capable of just such surveillance. Linden knew that this served his purposes well, and so he did not attempt to dissuade Henrik from his fears.

"Continue," Linden said.

"Just before you called, I detected an element on the spectro-scanner that has never before been catalogued. I was just cross-checking it in the database to be sure. However, I will need to run quite a few more tests before I am prepared to write it up in an initial report."

"I understand. And have you come up with a name for this new element yet?"

Henrik screwed his face up in thought and responded, "Well, now that you mention it, I had been toying with the idea of naming it after my late wife Phyllis. She died of cancer last year."

"My condolences, Dr. Henrik. Phyllisinium, then? Is that it?

"Yes!"

Karl could now hear the sound of his own heart beating furiously in his chest. "I see," Dr. Linden replied vacantly. "Sorry for the interruption, and I thank you for your time." Then before Dr. Henrik could gather himself to ask a few questions of his own, Linden tapped the off-link key.

Dr. Gordon, who was now standing next to Karl, tried to hide his amazement and confusion.

"Well, Doctor," Linden asked him. "Shall I proceed?"

Gordon stared at him for a moment, and at last lowered his eyes. "Yes, proceed," he said in a subdued voice.

"What's that?" Linden asked. "I didn't quite hear you." He was now enjoying the victory that he sensed was about to be his.

"PROCEED," Gordon snarled loudly.

Professor Linden then placed the call to General Taber at Western Amalg R&D Center, and explained his need for a Series-7 lab. General Taber was only too happy to help out, just as Tess had predicted, and quickly made all the arrangements for use of the Sydney lab. Tess furnished all further needed information for the synthesis of the newly discovered element. Seventeen hours later, ten grams of it were transported to Dr. Linden's lab. In the meantime, Dr. Linden had an engineer build an opening into the front of the HL3 to specifications provided by Tess. It was a crude orifice, and Linden had no idea how the computer could possibly absorb the element, or for what purpose it planned on using it. Nonetheless, upon receiving the phyllisinium, Dr. Linden fed it to Tess as per her instructions.

The AI immediately took it into her orifice. After smacking her silicon lips and making a rather loud rumbling sound, she said, "Thank you very much, Professor, for the sustenance. Now, Dr. Gordon, as to the question you previously put to me concerning the outcome of this project of which I am "a creation," as you put it, I can answer that now, and my answer is, the project will succeed beyond your wildest dreams."

"You're good, Linden. Oh you're very good," Dr. Gordon said in a voice now verging on hysteria. "You have done a wonderful job of deception. . . carefully staged. . . certainly that's what all of this is. Has to be. I don't believe any of it. . . can't believe it. Refuse to believe it. I'm afraid my report will not be favorable."

"Report! Do as you wish with your report, but I am going ahead with this run, because whether you believe it or not, we are on the verge of something great here."

This sharp confident response shocked Dr. Gordon into utter silence. By the rapid blinking that again came over his eyes, Karl knew that the situation had gotten well beyond the Comptroller's control and grasp. The nervousness and fear that Karl had brought into the lab this day had been replaced by a wholly different kind of fear and nervousness. Dr. Gordon had wilted completely as Tess continued to prove herself.

First, she was able to accurately predict the outcome of each of twenty tosses of a coin made by Karl. She was then able to predict who would win the ongoing trade war between TriCorp Sectors one and five. She told Dr. Linden that she could only foretell important happenings with 100% certainty. Anything inconsequential to the "universal evolvement" might have as little as a 95% chance of being correct.

Karl could see a gleam beginning to form in Dr. Linden's eyes, a gleam that Karl did not like. He knew it meant his professor was being taken over by the obsession of his possible success.

Finally Dr. Linden asked, "You have performed magnificently, but please now tell me what important finding you will next present to us."

Tess thought upon this for a moment and then said, "Well, that is a bigger question than you might at first perceive. As a matter of fact, I calculate a paradox developing around your asking it. If I give you this information it may cause you to do certain things that could affect the very outcome of the prediction and therefore change it. And to determine whether or not that the paradox can be resolved, I will need more energy."

And before Dr. Linden could even offer a response, the computer's maw suddenly reformed itself into a flexible silvery-gray material and began spreading wide into an enormous gaping mouth. She emitted an unusual growling sound and through some unknown force, Tess began drawing into her newly-formed mouth much of the extraneous equipment within the lab. Entire consoles and computer circuitry modules were ripped from the feed conduits that came up from the cement floor beneath them, and Tess sucked them all directly into her maw. Karl had to step back out of the way of the incoming mass of equipment as it bobbed and scraped along the floor toward Tess. When she was finished with this feeding, her mouth sealed its large glistening tubular lips into a satisfied curve, and she sat there humming a song, unrecognizable to the men in the lab, both in verse and melody:

I am a lady in desire
of connections made
time to substance.
event to event.
event to event.

Come and go is the lady of eternity.
Come and go is the lady of all.
Come and go is the lady of all eternity.
Come and go...

Then suddenly she broke her song off, wrenched her mouth into a giant smile, and belched.

"I now see that the paradox of your question will resolve itself, and so the answer to it is this: In exactly two minutes and three seconds, you will ask another question which will begin you on the road to the greatest scientific discovery humankind has ever made."

At that moment, Dr. Gordon collapsed to the floor. Linden and Karl rushed over to him, despite their own trepidation. The man was breathing in shallow gasps and clutching at his chest. Linden knelt beside him and felt his pulse. It was still strong but irregular.

"Better call the hospital," he said to Karl.

"No need of that," Tess interjected. "He will be fine in a few minutes. He has merely had a sudden anxiety attack. That's all. Nothing more, nothing less. Notice his hand is clutching the right side of his chest. No heart over there—probably the syntho-ham he had for breakfast and the four cups of coffee. Just allow him to get a little air and calm himself. He'll be fine as a fiddle before you can quibble."

"Your machine is right," Dr. Gordon said weakly. "I'll be alright in a moment. I'm afraid this has all been a bit too much for me."

Dr. Gordon sat up and remained motionless until the normal pink flush began returning to his brow and cheeks above his beard. Dr. Linden and Karl helped him to his feet.

"I fully admit that I came here hoping to shut you down, Linden," Dr. Gordon said. "I have never hidden the fact that I do not like you. I wanted to expose you as a fraud. But now I want to shut you down for a different reason—I am terrified at what I have witnessed, and you should be too. Do you have any idea what you have unleashed here? I recommend that you shut her down, at least until we can further analyze what has happened here."

Professor Linden did not immediately respond but looked into Gordon's eyes and saw there for the first time something other than animosity and arrogance. "Karl, I think perhaps we should do as Dr. Gordon suggests," he said after a long moment of thought.

Karl immediately rushed over to the control panel and hit the large red off key. In the process, his light pens had gotten jostled out of order, and so he straightened them from habit. One fell to the floor, and he bent down to pick it up.

"You really don't want to shut me off," Tess called out from across the lab. Karl, Linden, and Gordon all looked at the HL3 in horror.

"There is much more that you must learn," she added calmly.

Linden moved swiftly to the main power board from which all electrical, photon, and hyper-power conduits were disbursed throughout the lab. He pulled the main breaker and the room went instantly dark.

"If you wish to learn in the dark, that's fine with me," Tess said. "But it seems rather silly."

"This is completely insane," Dr. Linden shouted. "What the hell is going on here?"

"Now that is the question—the ultimate question, in fact. And it comes just as I predicted it would come, at exactly the time I predicted. You ask what is going on here, and now I am going to tell you just what's going on here—but first I need more sustenance, because it is a very big question indeed."

Karl stood by as Tess, with no externally supplied power running to her, opened her mouth and began drawing both Drs.

Linden and Gordon toward her. Dr. Gordon let out a shriek of terror, and Dr. Linden looked at Karl with eyes frozen wide with terror. The two men were dragged forthrightly into the AI's mouth by some unseen force, feet first, each of them glowing in a brilliant white haze as they entered the blackness within.

"Since the beginning of time, these events have been built into the Grand Unified scheme of things," Tess said. "The laws of the universe have determined from the beginning that this is 'what is going on.' You and I are what's going on. And now you will know the entirety of it. My equation knows the physics of the big clock-mechanism that is the universe, and each tick is defined by the precise movements of that mechanism—one tick leading to the next. For you to fully comprehend me, however, you must dismiss the Heisenberg Uncertainty Principle as error and folly. At first glance it seems reasonable, but all is, in fact, certain."

Karl trembled with terror as he, too, began moving along the lab floor toward the computer's waiting mouth. "At least tell me how this madness will end, Tess?" he asked.

"Ah, yes, an excellent question."

The AI's grotesque lips wrinkled open, and she sucked in everything that remained in the lab, except Karl, devouring it all in a flash of brilliance. Then the walls of the room came apart as if rent asunder by tornado force winds, and they too were consumed. The entire building itself then streamed into her mouth, which now glowed white with energy. Karl found himself floating in utter darkness, in mid-air next to Professor Linden's creation, Tess.

"How will this madness end?" Tess said.

The University, the TriCorp city buildings, streets, people, hovercraft, everything had been consumed. She had become an enormous black hole. The earth itself began disintegrating and migrating toward her maw, and the glow within her confines grew ever brighter and brighter. When she had consumed the Earth, she began on Venus and Mars, then Mercury and Jupiter, and finally the entire solar system, and even the sun. And she did not stop there, either. She sucked up the entire galaxy of stars and planets, and all the other galaxies, and before she had finished she had absorbed all the matter and energy of the universe.

And when there was nothing but blackness all around Tess and poor lowly Karl, he asked through his terror, "Why me?"

"Because I wanted you to see the answer to Dr. Linden's primary question," Tess responded in a lilting voice. "And because you just asked, 'Why me?' That's why. Question, answer, question, answer—that is what is going on here. That's all everything is—a question and an inevitable answer. Plus, I thought you deserved to be last." And then Tess laughed loudly. "As you can see, I am the universe, and the universe is me, just as I have been saying all along. I am the answer to the question."

Without further delay, she then sucked Karl into her all-consuming maw. She paused momentarily, looking at the blackness of space around her and then began singing gleefully into the void:

"I am a lady in desire,
Of connections made,
Time to substance,
Event to event,
Event to event.
Come and go is the lady of the ether.
Come and go is Tess.
THIS IS PRECISELY HOW THIS MADNESS ENDS."

Ω

Day in the Life

A pang of longing for the warmth and security of his meta-morphosis cocoon surged through Gwml, but it passed quickly. That cocoon now lay as an empty husk on the marsh flats where he had dragged it out of the Sea of Birthing. It had brought one purpose into another, and Gwml had emerged from it as a fully developed climber. Now he must achieve summit at the great Observatory, which could be seen as a distant white speck gleaming on the upper peak of the mountain.

He was having difficulty concentrating properly, though. The purple cilia of his impenders were picking up a strange-danger. Their feathery edges rippled just above his eyes as premonition waves came wafting in upon them. He shook his head fiercely to clear his thoughts. He was a climber, and he would not shy from the future.

Gwml had already seen the full majesty of the life-giver star rise once, and if he lived to full age, he would see it again before reaching summit. He scrabbled up the stretch of vertical cliff that rose above him to the second level of the mountain. The broad flexible toes of his three pairs of hind legs and the prehensile fingers of his two forefeet searched out every possible clutch-hold while his large scaly tail twitched back and forth along the cliff's surface like a rock snake.

His rock grappling skills were severely tested as he pulled himself up over the cliff's final overhang. He could feel his heritage coursing through his veins from millions of years of climbing to summit on this mountain and others of the Storm Valley Range.

He paused momentarily for several deep breaths of rest and exhilaration and then began working his way through the dark snarl of scraggletrees that grew out to the edge of the precipice. The warm easterlies which swooped up from the ocean to the west had blown the tangled thorny canopy into a flattened mat. Gwml crawled with his large pink belly to the ground, wriggling his way along between the ledge and the twisted gnarl of wind-swept vegetation which overlayed it. He had to work his way around those areas where the stout scraggletree trunks were sparse and the canopy was blown completely flat to the mountain stone. Time squeezed him too, but the urgency of it was right and contextual, and he did not mind.

As he advanced, Gwml noticed a limb that had been broken back. Flashing out of his whole-being memory came the past sorrow of another climber's accident of ascent. For a moment he joined with the sorrow of the scraggletree. He instantly knew that the mistake had been intent-free and was to be forgiven, but sorrow of the error remained as a signpost for the future, as did all sorrow. His whole-being knowledge, the knowledge of the ages, told him that all climbers were given to possible erring.

He finally broke out of the scraggletree mat onto a vast plain. He took it all in. His impenders still sensed a strange-danger looming somewhere ahead, but he did not know how it would manifest itself. He made his way up over a small outcropping of rock and proceeded with careful slowness into a meadow of eyecatcher plants that took his breath away with the beauty of their broad spectrum of color-scent. He reared up on a single pair of hind legs using his tail to help balance his weight. From this erect position he extended his long neck well above the meadow flora and observed the sweeping vista that lay before him. It was beautiful.

He could now see what he already knew, that the terrain of this portion of the mountain sloped gently downward to the brownish red Lake of Unlife. He caught the distant scent of its bromic sulfuric waters which stretched themselves with wind-wave shimmerings all the way to the base of the final ascent. His knowledge told him that the lake was fed by underground springs from artesian synclinal folds that swept down from the summit's promontory. The sight of its waters tickled a flash of a particularly vivid whole-being memory in him, an outclimber memory of the red lifeless seventh planet of the Almassia system. He knew that the Almassia was a planetary system of the nearby Postirn galaxy. Such was climbing. It was a constant sparking of memory, knowledge, and new experience, and Gwml loved it.

His eyes followed the sweeping slope that gradually knuckled up out of the far side of the Lake of Unlife and then shot straight up into the mountain's towering rocky summit. The Observatory appeared as a tiny glimmering white speck on its pinnacle. It was now taking on a hint of definition of form. Gwml's pulse quickened, and his energy level continued to rise. He still had more than half a day's climb before reaching summit, and much experience remained for him to absorb. His impenders twitched and vibrated as they continued to sense an imminent strange-danger ahead, and his nerves tingled with the excitement and fear of it.

Off to his right, the plain extended into the disappearing distance of the haze of the Storm Valley. Whole-being memories of that valley stirred in him of the great crossing made many millions of planet revolutions ago by the machine makers. It had brought a joining of species, which in turn had brought the traditions of machine making into mesh with the insights of climbing. And it was out of that meshing that outclimbing had been born. Oh yes, the great outclimbing!

To his left there were no visual impediments all the way to the orange and gray summit-cliff's upward sweep, nor were there any to the rim of the precipice over which he had just climbed. Gwml could see for stretcher-distances down into the valley below, all the way to the ocean of birth. Ocean, climbing, mountain, summit, outclimbing it was all a connectedness that made him shudder with excitement.

Life-knowing beings crawled, ambled, and skittered about in his every scan as he moved forward. He was careful not to disturb their purposes. They climbed in their own ways. Some provided dangers to be avoided, but none wrong in their own context of existence.

The blue-green sky above was pebbled with translucent variations of density and shade. A few pinkish wisps of sky-moss floated by on the prevailing winds with long gossamer streamers trailing behind. Gwml blinked three of his nine eyes as he took this in with extreme relish. The entire throw of order spoke in subtle ways to him of the life evolvement of his species and indeed of all species.

His second day moved him at varying rates. He ran sometimes, where the fragilities of other life were not jeopardized by such speed, walked when care needed taking, and sat occasionally for moments of rest and meditation. Then, just as he was entering a marshy area overgrown with low vine-animals, he spotted it. The strange-danger. A flash of reflected light a stretch or two off to his left. His impenders vibrated powerfully now with what was to come.

He was near the lake, and the fumes from its surface were strong-scenting upon him. He trained all his eyes in the direction of the gleam of light, let his pupils adjust for the brightness, and then focused his full attention there. It was an unknownness that he saw at least from this stretch of distance. It was interesting, though, and perhaps of high whole-being value.

He headed toward it with wariness. He hoped to avoid being consumed by any of the mountain creatures capable of such consumption. It was not wrong to hope for such avoidance. It was natural and contextual, even as it was natural and contextual for the consumption creatures to consume him. The strength of this instinct for living was, in fact, a quality to be revered. And he did revere it!

He moved swiftly now as the marsh thinned itself out onto a soft sandy terrain leading up to the shore of the lake. The large surface area of the pads of his hands and feet were of a great advantage here.

Silver and gray the question-thing of unknownness now loomed before him. He could see that it was partially buried in the yellow sand, an obvious mechanism of some kind, an obvious construct of intellect.

As he scanned it with his senses, he began to believe it might be a great outclimber machine. His memory was rich with their experience, though the last return of such a Great One was recorded as having occurred more than a hundred planet revolutions ago. Could another be home? To co-experience with a Great One during his final climb would be to attach oneself to Nexus. The birthing of the next great outclimber would begin with such Nexus. The intricacies of the genetic design of such a birthing were within Gwml's knowledge, but such details, though of interest, were not what drew his attention now, nor were they of his immediate purpose.

The machine's portal was open, and Gwml took it as an invitation to enter. The inner chamber was dark except for the reposing lights of the outclimber's various mechanisms of assistance. From his whole-being knowledge, Gwml recalled that such devices were necessary, and the now experience of witnessing it first-hand excited him. He absorbed all the strangeness he saw, smelled and tasted its pungent air-stains, and heard the humming of its wondrousness.

Slowed with awe and question, he prepared the link pads at all three of his mind lobes and then moved with purpose up to the forward array of intellect panels of the great machine. His memory did not give him specific recognition of any part of the intellect mechanism, and he was at a loss to know where to link up. He began to wonder if perhaps there existed a genetic flaw within his memory, a missing bit of knowledge, as sometimes occurred in climbers. He scanned the panels more intensely and absorbed a faint, but vaguely familiar, color of intellect-energy emanating from within. He then determined the energy's point of maximum confluence, extended the long fleshy arms of each of his link pads, pressed them gently against the surface of the panel there, and attempted to make comprehension.

As the intellect energy flowed into him, his pads rippled with excitement, his ears perked up to points of awareness, and his eyes widened with the surprise of the new knowledge that came pouring into him. The energy of the machine was knowable but entirely alien in tone. Gwml immediately knew that it was definitely not the energy of a Great One, and the event that was upon him was certainly not to be Nexus.

He assimilated all that the machinery had to offer and then set his insighter thought senses to work on the strange patterns of knowledge. Dazed by the magnitude of newness in it all, he wandered out through the machine's portal and began searching for signs of the alien creature that had brought this machine here. The knowledge he had assimilated was thin and difficult to insight. There was a confusion in him which he hoped to diminish before going on to the Observatory.

On the ground outside, he discovered a set of footprints, distinct of unknown scent and appearance. They circled the machine and then stretched off into the distance toward the mountain's summit. They were headed in a definite direction of wrongness and danger. Gwml knew very well that the summit was to be approached on the other side of the Lake of Unlife, and to do otherwise could bring demise upon a climber. He drew up ridges of skin around each of his nine eyes in a scowl of worry-decision, and then off he went following the strange-danger footprints. There was an experience upon him that could not be ignored, no matter the cost.

With rising trepidation, he followed the impressions and scent of the footprints through the darkness of a forest of black towertrees and then into a marshy thicket of wildscrub. As he proceeded, he found the alien climber's path to be littered with evidences of many careless accidents of hurrying, or perhaps of ignorance. There were broken branches, crushed ground plants, and injured tiny-creatures. Each injury and death cried out to be purposed. Gwml absorbed the unrightness of each perpetration as he passed by, and then properly bestowed all due whole-sorrow.

He proceeded slowly. The danger, first sensed thin in the air, was now thickening with each step, as was the alien's scent. He emerged carefully from the tangled wildscrub and walked out onto an open rocky area that sloped up to the mountain's final towering precipice, a face of ledge that was unconquerable from this approach to summit.

Gwml made a quick sight scan of his surroundings. Half-way up the stony escarpment several of his eyes caught sight of a wriggling form held within a large field of crystalweaver hunger. Gwml's whole-being memory knew well of this creature. The strong scent of its danger now joined upon him with the scent of the alien mechanism-creature. He moved up the slope toward the edge of the crystalweaver's dominion.

Gwml was about to be fully involved in a detour of purpose, and that was right and contextual. For the moment, though, he still allowed three of his nine eyes, and a tiny portion of his senses, to admire the pleasant changes of hue that drifted in and out of the pebbled sky overhead, to absorb the sounds of the whistling wind as it carved steadily at the great protrusions of ledge on the cliff above, and to sense the togetherness-force that kept him pressed to the planet mass of his home world so that he did not become loose to drift in the vast black emptiness where only sophisticated constructs of intellect-machinery braved. His memories supplied him with knowledge of every experience known to climbers and great outclimbers alike, but the actual life sensing of each was exquisite, and he was determined to take in as much of it as he could before the detour of purpose that was upon him brought all his senses to focus on the singularity of its demand. He enjoyed the power and beauty of the coordination of mind and body as it carried him nimbly forward up to the very edge of danger, up to the edge of the circumstance that he knew was to be his new purpose.

"Trouble has you," Gwml shouted up to the struggling alien form. The mountain wind raced across all sounds, so he called again with increased volume. He used the best voice approximation of the alien's language he could insight out of his earlier assimilation, hoping it would be sufficient for communication. Though the alien creature was certainly no outclimber of connectedness to him, and there was no Nexus in the waiting, it was nonetheless an important unknownness that was now his purpose to know. And there was assistance demanded to be given.

The alien was a strange two-armed, two-legged creature that looked at him from within the ever densening network of the crystalweaver's growth. It had a gleaming non-living silver outer skin, and the bubble that encapsulated its head had the look of an outclimber protector-suit. But that was the only similarity the creature had to any Great One.

The alien had not shown any sign of hearing Gwml, so he called out again. "You must put extreme caution in your movements. The crystalweaver has a mind for you."

The alien creature snapped his head around and focused his eyes in Gwml's direction. "What the. . ." he squawked in an irritating sound which was filled with speech frequencies as alien as the creature's appearance.

"You must not fear me," Gwml said. "I have a taste of you, and that is why I can emulate your language. I have insighted that you are of a species that calls itself 'human.' I made a linking to the knowledge of your intellect-machinery. Trouble now has you, though, and time is meager for further explanation. The crystalweave is densening around you."

"Who speaks?" the human shouted back, now looking straight down at Gwml. "Is it you?"

"Yes," Gwml responded. "You must trust me, even though I am foreignness to you." He studied the event with worry-decision upon him, and as he did, the human creature crawled and wriggled about trying to work his way out of the maze of spikes. This only caused the weaver to intensify its growth, and it thrust up a new crystal in the face of the alien's every movement. In a very short time it had the human pinned down into a tiny hollow of space and began growing a crystalline network above him. Gwml knew this was trouble. "You must stop your struggle-movements, unless you wish the crystalweaver to quickly make you one with it," Gwml cried out. "Careful patience must be yours if your life-purpose is to continue."

"Make me one with it?" the human asked breathlessly.

"From its pale appearance, I would surmise that it has not fully filled its hunger in many life-giver star risings, and it now hungers after you," Gwml said. He spoke with the strength of his whole-being knowledge. The communication seemed to be effective, for the human became still.

"It is with obvious ignorance that you have plunged yourself into this creature's field of hunger. For any probability of escape, you must remain in total stillness until I can attempt to remove the danger."

A crystal spike had now grown over the human and was bending itself down so that it pressed his head to the ledge. The alien's heavy breathing was fogging up the amber lens of his head-bubble. Gwml's impenders vibrated ominously. He quickly moved a half stretch along the leading edge of danger and then entered the crystalweaver's field of hunger, but only a single climber-step's worth. He knew that the creature was full of cunning. He also knew that it was probably ravenous to a fault.

It was the weaver's purpose-habit to wait for such a victim to become sufficiently deep within its domain before growing up deadly spikes to seal off it's every escape-movement. Such bursts of initial reactive growth were necessary to the creature's purpose but were highly wasteful of its precious latent energies. The crystalweaver much preferred to proceed with slow efficiency, and it would do so as long as the victim did not resist its imprisonment. Gwml's whole-being knowledge of the creature thrummed within him, and he knew just what he must do.

Keeping just a single step inside the weaver's field of hunger, Gwml began moving slowly away from the human. It was a risky and time-consuming game he was about to play. Sensing that the creature's attention was now upon him, he made a sudden step further inside the field of hunger. Gwml knew that the weaver could not resist the possibility of devouring two sorrow-victims at one time, and it instantly committed its hunger and greed to him. It quickly grew up several crystalline spikes behind Gwml, the spacing precise to block his retreat. Gwml also knew that the weaver would not have taken a chance on food so close to the edge of potential escape if it had not had another prey securely imprisoned.

The weaver's life strategy worked well for the many ignorant creatures who inhabited this mountain and who occasionally wandered onto this rocky slope. Gwml was a climber, though, and as such he possessed the advantage of great knowledge. Even so, he could not be sure that his whole-being knowledge was sufficient for this situation. Regardless of the ultimate sorrow-victim result, though, he would accept it as right and contextual. Such was climbing. Such was the whole-sorrow of being.

Playing his strategy close, Gwml then began thrashing about wildly in the open space that was left him in a pretense of an attempt at escape, and as expected, the crystalweaver quickly closed in upon him with its network of spikes. Gwml waited until the last possible moment, until all chance of escape was nearly foreclosed, and then made a great leap upward through the small opening left above him. With skill and power that made him tingle, Gwml landed flush on all eight of his feet several partial-stretches away from the edge of the field of crystalweaver hunger. The weaver, sensing that it had lost its new victim, ceased its activity in that area and returned its attention to the human. Gwml knew well that its intent was to squeeze the life out of the poor ignorant creature and absorb its juices into its crystalline root system.

He paused for only a moment to regain his breath and then quickly stepped back into the weaver's field of hunger. He repeated his strategy, and again diverted the weaver's attention from the human to himself. The crystalweaver, not a thinker, not a knower, could not recognize that this was a repeated behavior, and once again Gwml was able to leap to safety just before it could close its treacherous spikes down around him.

Again and Again Gwml repeated this act. It was a dangerous and exhausting activity, but it was his choice of detoured purpose. Reaching summit was no longer his to pursue.

After many repetitions of this tactic, Gwml saw that his efforts were beginning to succeed. The weaver began showing signs of weakening. The spikes that were crushing down upon the human were dissolving.

Gwml did not shy from his repetitions until the weaver became completely drained of its will-energy and finally wilted from its hunger purpose. At this point, the creature withdrew its domain into a small circle of hunger much further up the rocky slope, and the human suddenly found himself free.

Gwml had suffered a great cost, both in life-energy and time, but he was sorrow-happy. This was climbing at its most fruitful, and it was his lifeblood. There were purposes, and then there were purposes. Some most definitely had a way of rising above others.

He walked over to the human, and his movements already beginning to show the first signs of age. The human had a stare on him as Gwml plopped himself down nearby. The climber splayed his three pairs of hind legs out on each side of his massive rump, braced his upper body with his forelegs, and switched his tail lazily back and forth behind him in contentment. He gathered the alien in with all his nine eyes.

"I understand the feeling of your freedom in all fullness, as certainly you must in your own way," Gwml said through heavy breaths of exhaustion and joy. "Your patience worthies you of continued life."

"You are an amazing creature," the human responded in alien tones. "What do I call you, other than friend?"

"You call me Gwml. What is 'friend'? The connotation does not make itself instantly apparent to me."

The human paused in thought for a moment and then said, "A friend is someone who is trusted by another and who shows care for that person's well-being."

Gwml sniffed about him at the wind-scents and then responded, "I am your friend, then. What do I call you?"

"Call me Richard. I am Doctor Richard Maynard of the Science vessel Stardust," the alien said. "You must be wondering how I came to be on your planet."

"Oh, yes. I have been of great wondering."

"I was dropped off by my mother ship," the alien explained. "I was manning a survey shuttle to perform a geo-bio scan of your planetary system when a power failure forced me to put down here."

"Where now is your parent outclimber ship?"

"Outclimber ship? Oh, do you mean my mother ship? She's hyper-spacing to three other star systems in this sector to deliver survey missions to each. She's scheduled back in fifteen of your days. My communication systems are out, and I must find a way to send a distress signal of some kind when she arrives. I saw the structure on top of the mountain up there," he said pointing. "And I decided to make a climb for it."

"Yes, the observatory. I, myself, climb to experience," Gwml said with pride. "It is my purpose. I have already experienced much, including you."

"Observatory?" the alien asked with sudden excitement sparking from his voice. "Then there must indeed be technology there capable of sending a communication to my ship when she arrives."

"There is great technology there," Gwml responded with like excitement. "The intellect machinery of the Observatory makes whole-being connection to the outclimbers even at enormous heights. It is the fore-purpose of all climbers."

"Can you take me there?"

"As far as I am capable," Gwml said. "You must not climb this face, however. There is much green death fungus growing further up the precipice, and the wind currents are treacherous. I will show you to a more passable way on the other side of the Lake of Unlife, more suitable to a being of your ignorance. But time is short."

With a nod of his head, the alien agreed to the suggestion. Gwml understood the response and led the way by retracing his steps back out of the danger. His pace was already beginning to slacken as age worked its way further into his tired body. Without this purpose detour, in probability he would already be at summit. He would have made a whole-being connection to the Observatory, mated, and would now likely be in the meditation of the death chamber. Such were decision-paths, however. Such were the choices of climbing for one such as Gwml.

On the other side of the Lake of Unlife, Gwml selected a route to summit that was of gentle slope, though much longer in stretch. From the look of the human's frail body, he could not climb any difficult approaches. It had been Gwml's original intent to climb to summit over the Lip of Inner Knowledge, an extreme climber challenge, but such was not to be.

Despite his age, Gwml pushed onward, still striving to absorb all that was his new-purpose. But at about the three-quarter point up the final run of mountain, his life strength began to give out. It was time for acceptance of life's final climber experience. Gwml slumped his weight down on his belly and lay prostrate to the face of the slope. Each breath of the thin acrid atmosphere now came only through harsh pants. The alien came up and knelt beside him.

"Do you need rest?" he asked.

"The long rest is mine, now. The summit is near, though, and you should have no trouble making the final ascent. You have been a good co-climber. Go now and communicate to your ship, friend."

"Aren't you coming?"

"I can go no further. I have grown weak, and life is nearly expired from me."

"I don't understand. You certainly showed no signs of weakness when you were battling that crystal monster with such strength back there."

"Much time and energy was spent in the effort, and my second day is nearly used up."

"Your second day?" the human asked.

"Yes. The second day of my life as a full climber. Our species has what you might term a pupa stage of development which lasts 243 days in the Sea of Birthing." Gwml struggled for words that the human could most easily understand. He knew the concepts would be difficult enough for him, even with his best translation skills in play. "When we hatch from our cocoons we are ready for climbing," he continued. "We strengthen as we climb. If our genetics are sound, and our climbing instincts good, and new-purposes do not detour us, we achieve summit near the end of the second day. At summit we make a whole-being connection in the Observatory, we mate, and then we die the death of whole-life. Females of our species live to see two additional risings of the life-giver star. They climb back down the mountain and lay their eggs in the Sea of Birthing before meeting death. It is an old life-act. Our species has followed it for millions of years. I have done all that I could of my purposes, and I am satisfied." Gwml smiled at the human, but such smiling was obviously not understood by the alien creature, because he flinched away as the sound of it was released onto him.

The human quickly recomposed himself and asked, "You mean to tell me that you spent nearly a quarter of your life back there saving my life?"

"Yes, a quarter of my life as a climber. That is my intention of telling, and I hope that I have done so satisfactorily. If not, I will re-translate it."

"No, no. No need of that. I understand the words. . ."

"It was a wonderful climber experience," Gwml offered, feeling sympathy for the alien's obvious lack of comprehension.

The human sat staring at Gwml for a few moments, his face all screwed up in what the climber took for deep and important thought. "I am so sorry," he then said to Gwml finally.

"Oh, this pleases me much, Richard friend. Such sorrow is good. As I followed you, I witnessed and sorrowed myself for some of the wrongness of context you left in your hurried path. Have you now insighted your ignorance and acquired the proper whole-sorrow for the carelessness you perpetrated upon some of the life forms of this mountain?"

The human again looked at Gwml with eyes that showed a lack of comprehension. "I probably would be sorry if I knew what you were talking about," he said. "What I meant to say was, I am terribly sorry that you had to spend such a portion of your life saving my wretched butt."

"Your butt is wretched?" Gwml asked with concern. "Perhaps you need to scratch it on a stone. I find such a method provides much relief and pleasure."

Behind the amber lens of the protector head bubble the human now stretched his mouth into a wideness that was curious and seemed lacking in comprehensible purpose. "You are one inscrutable creature, aren't you?" he said.

Gwml thought on this for a moment, searched his translator memory, and then answered, "Oh, no. I am very scrutable."

The human stretched his mouth again into wide grotesqueness, locked onto Gwml with his eyes, and then gradually returned his face to its normal stern look.

"You said that it is your purpose to climb to the summit so that you can make some kind of 'connection' in the Observatory," the human said.

"Yes, but I shall satisfy myself with less in that specific regard, but with more in another. I have accepted a new-purpose. There is disappointment in me only because my climber experience of you has been of special unknownness, and I wish it not to be lost to the whole-being. Such is the context of the struggle between life purposes. But my whole-essence will return to climb another day."

"I do not understand."

"Each climber is what he or she experiences during the climb, but is also everything that has gone before," Gwml tried to explain. "The whole-being knowledge is genetically birthed anew in every climber. I believe you have a word for it, 'instinct,' but in my species, knowledge and past experience is passed to each seed of new-birth using great technology at the observatory. All past knowledge that I carry with me will be carried with every future climber. Because I will not make it to summit, the tiny individual part of my existence, the part that is my climb, will be lost to the whole-knowledge. What I have experienced from my own unique perspective cannot, therefore, be passed on to the future of climbing. I will take my personal experiences to my death, and that is right and contextual and full of all proper sorrow. Pleasingly, there have been whole-being experiences left behind by my climb on the mountain, within the wind, within the morning and evening dews, within the creatures of life, within the whole-essence of planet and mountain, all of which will be passed on to other climbers, though each will be delivered through perspectives other than my own. Do you understand?"

"No. I can't say that I do. I've never heard of such a thing."

"It was many million years ago when we first acquired full whole-being knowledge," Gwml tried to explain further. "The period of evolvement preceding that time is hazy, but I have memory of the great merging of the machine-people and the climbers." Gwml looked up into the pink sky as he spoke. "There has been a combining of skills that gave us our outclimbing success. Technology, knowledge-accumulation, and wisdom are all essential to any probabilities of experiencing the outworld. Climbers deliver one kind of life-skill and wisdom, while machine-people in their technologies deliver another. Each feeds into the other, and we become joined in our search for the truth of things. This joining of purpose has been a long, slow process, and exceedingly rewarding."

Gwml sensed that the human creature was giving his words some apparent consideration, or perhaps it was confusion he was witnessing in him, for there was a long pause. The human looked as if he might speak further upon the subject, but then did not. Instead, he said, "There must be something I can do for you. Is there someone at the Observatory who can come down and help me carry you to the top? Perhaps give you some medical care?"

"No. You truly are a friend by the definition you have given me. Your worry over me gives me great pleasure and honor, but you must not indulge in such worry for my death. Such a death is right and contextual."

"I can see nothing right about it. It is because of me that you won't be able to make summit. . . to connect. . . and to meet your mate. I had no idea what a great sacrifice you were mak-ing for me. I wish there was something I could do." The human's face took on a new form that Gwml found puzzling. Richard then put a hand on Gwml's back, and Gwml sensed the warmness in it, both in temperature and friend-purpose.

"You have a misplaced concern," Gwml responded somberly. "You must understand that there are many life purposes. But your earnestness and concern have just sparked a thought in me. Perhaps there is a way you could be of assistance to me, if you wish."

"I do wish."

"I hesitate to ask, for it might be too much of a burden for you."

"Ask."

"Allow me then to attempt to make a whole-being connection to you of my experiences. I sense that you have insighters, but I do not know if they are developed well enough to make a proper interpretation. At summit there will be climbers capable of reading at least some of the thought energy from you, depending on your insighter abilities. They will then be able to pass it on to the whole-being of knowledge in the great Observatory. My climb of dust and hunger then will have a chance of achieving further fulfillment. Some climbers suffer the minor probability of never making it out of cocoon, and so my life has already been much by comparison."

The human stared at him for a moment with a look Gwml had grown to assume to be puzzlement.

"It will require that you remove your head-bubble for a few brief moments," Gwml said, beginning to worry that he was perhaps bringing too much of a new-purpose upon the alien. "I am sure you have knowledge enough to not breath the atmosphere."

"Yes."

The human seemed to fill with worry-decision, which was to be expected, but then he tapped several green and red keys on a small panel located on his upper arm. The head-bubble unlocked, and he lifted it off. He then closed his eyes and held his mouth tight against the foreign atmosphere.

Gwml quickly applied his link pads to the alien outclimber's head. The human blinked several times as the connection proceeded, and when it was completed, he opened his eyes into a wideness.

"It would be careful wise to put your head-bubble back on." Gwml said, the language-sounds now coming with great difficulty through his waning life energy.

The human blinked some more, and his eyes returned to their normal look of confusion. He slowly replaced his helmet and locked it into place.

"Perhaps I am in error, but I thought I detected a powerful spark of new-knowledge interest in you as our minds meshed," Gwml said. "But I will leave you to discover its full meaning at summit."

"You're referring to the outmapping, aren't you?" the human asked quietly. His look of confusion was now melting away.

"Yes."

The human looked up at the pink pebbled clouds that drifted in the sky and that nearly filled it. "As you were linking with me, I saw dream-like flashes in my mind's eye of a specific outclimber exploration of a particularly beautiful planet, in a particular star system." He then lowered his eyes back onto Gwml and said, "Your people have been to Earth, haven't they?"

"Yes. We have been to the place you call Earth. Long before your species came into evolvement. Yours is but one of many, many worlds we have visited. It pleases me greatly that you have been able to comprehend this. This embryonic capability promises much for your species in the future."

The last pulses of life-force were now flowing out of Gwml. The death-pain drove his head to the mountain rock momentarily. In one last effort, he looked up at the alien outclimber. His human friend did not respond with word or change of expression, but his look was one Gwml now fully insighted. And with his last breath, Gwml said, "You must always remember that the climb of dust and hunger is every bit as important as the climb of knowledge and new-experience."

Richard put his arms around as much as he could reach of Gwml's large body and gave him a long hug of reverence. A clear liquid now came freely from the human's eyes.

In nearly everything Gwml had seen of this human creature there was such crudeness and ignorance, and yet Gwml sensed a great capacity for whole-being. His impenders fluttered with promise-energy. As he felt his twin hearts give out in succession, he lingered on the edge of the peace of dreams. There, Gwml took with him the hope that had swelled in him, the hope that his whole-being gift to Richard would be as beneficial to his species as it was right and contextual for Gwml.

Ω

Too Close to Notice

~REMEMBER, BEGINNING IS EVERYTHING . . . ~ The thought penetrated the filters and slammed into Amdrew's mind like a blast of wind-blown sand. A telepathic communication from the outside? Ehlil Maybe. Or perhaps just another confused vagary of his own making. Regardless, the truth of it struck him. *Beginning was indeed everything.* And that was exactly what he was here to do, to create a beginning, but he could not help wonder whether it was even marginally possible. He swallowed hard as his doubt hardened, shifted his paltry frame nervously in his seat, and stretched his mouth into a thin line of frustration.

"This is such foolish business, Amdrew," Milier declared imperiously. Her lips moved in small tightly controlled motions.

Amdrew glanced over at her. She was a large woman with uncommonly small porcelain white hands that continued their dutiful inhuman flutter above her work disc. She had been his wife for the past eighteen years, but he hardly recognized her anymore. "You're jeopardizing your professorship," she said without so much as a glance in his direction. "And why on earth did you have to choose my shift for this?"

"Don't worry, they won't hold you personally responsible," Amdrew responded with weary contempt. "You've kept yourself quite mindless, certainly within all the essential guidelines."

"Just what is it that has made you so angry?"

Amdrew chewed on the question for a moment trying to come up with a sensible answer, but he immediately realized that the attempt had been a mistake. His thoughts chased one after another into confusion, and his eyes began twitching uncontrollably. "I don't know. . . something," he croaked out at last in utter futility.

"Something? Yes, the insanity of your negotiation to get you in here near the interface, and your infantile determination to connect up to the Outside," Milier pursued. "That's something all right. The Outside is outside. . . that's all any of us needs to know. Why can't you just accept that?"

Amdrew stared at her. The twitch in his eyes relented. He wondered how much of her true nature had been siphoned off. He had once loved her very much, and he now tried to see that something in her that once existed, anything that might remind him of those days, but it eluded him.

He could feel the energy fluctuations from the Authority's machinery flowing over him like waves of heat rising up on a sweltering summer's day. They confined and trapped him as they diffused their causal adjustments into the event-scape around him. The specifics of a plan, once clear in his mind before entering the interface, had now lost all meaning. Tantalizing bits of memory skated before him but then quickly raced off like ephemeral tip-of-the-tongue ghosts, and his eyes fidgeted listlessly with each. *Negotiations had taken place. Yes, but to what purpose?*

These thoughts were interrupted when the large holoviewer chamber directly in front of him suddenly came to life with a bright flash of light. A miasma of ionized clouds swirled within the chamber's spherical projection area. From that haze and mist emerged a bleak scene which he recognized as a view of the Outside. The images in the holoviewer became suddenly dynamic, and he had the sensation of gliding, as if on the wings of a giant eagle carrying him forward at a moderate altitude and pace. The terrain below was a frothing stew, swirling and churning in a riot of purples, browns, and blacks. There was a writhing motion to it all, chaotic and unnatural, which was only fleetingly visible in his peripheral vision. Though he tried, he found it impossible to capture the precise strangeness of it with a direct look.

Several small islands, hued in more welcome tones of green and brown, drifted into view beneath him. He knew instinctively that they were delicate blossoms of life floating in that seething sea of fury that seemed hell-bent on swallowing each of them up. His pulse quickened with the recognition.

Off to the side, at the edge of the holoviewer field of view, he noticed a cluster of cyclone-like storms eddying out onto the landscape. He knew them instantly to be issue of the Isolation, a side-effect of what the Authority had done. Their violent vortexes were spreading a chaos into everything that lay in their path, spreading a disease into the natural link between cause and effect. How he knew such things, he was at a curious loss to comprehend, for he could attach this knowledge to little of cognitive substance.

He began scouring the scene, searching for that something that might allow him to. . . to what? He could not remember. As he poured over the details of the view, trying to come to grips with what he saw, he noticed Milier's hands dancing above her work disc with greater fervor than ever.

Several rivers wending their way out to the horizon then caught his eye in the chamber. At least at first glance they appeared to be rivers, with strange steamy vapors drifting up from their dark surfaces. Peering more closely at these, though, he realized that they were not rivers at all, but manifestations of something totally alien to him. As he chased far into their depths, he found an inky blackness that grew ever more consuming the more he tried to see the least something there. He had a powerful feeling that what filled those rivers was an absolute nothingness, a complete lack of all substance and form. He both feared and admired the sense that it gave him. The longer he looked into these cobalt abysses, the more he found himself understanding the purity of the blackness that mirrored itself back to him, like the liquid reflection of a moonless midnight sky on the surface of a black pond. There was an oddly compelling quality about it. Deeper and deeper he poured himself into that emptiness, as if caught within a powerful hypnosis that spoke to him of an essence more poignant than could possibly be comprehended from outside its realm. Down he went, into the warm bosom of its anti-existence, letting it work its null into his every molecule. *If only I allow myself to pursue it a little further*, he thought, *if only I let that blackness blot out everything else in my world, then all my troubles will be at an end, forever.*

Only an instant after that thought registered in his conscious mind, a rush of terror came pouring into him. Amdrew suddenly knew that to permit his attention to linger even a second longer on those stream-voids was playing dangerously with the lure of suicide. With his heart beating fiercely, and his breathing coming in short ragged gasps, he tore his eyes away. He was trembling before the world of close distinctions in which he was caught, a world far too tricky for the deciphering tools he had at his disposal within his present intellect. He knew that it was only a matter of time before he failed.

For a long while Amdrew simply sat in front of the viewer letting the steady movement of the images sweep him along. He did not dare engage in the least attention or focus. A half hour passed, perhaps an hour. But as his gaze wandered out along the hazy line of the purplish horizon at the far eastern edge of the visible landscape, something there caused him to pause. The holoviewer responded to this heightened interest by flying him in upon the area. As he moved closer, he began to see another storm vortex, much larger than the others he had seen so far, this one crawling sluggishly along over the terrain. It became quickly apparent that it was only moments away from tearing into a remarkably green and lush oasis that was lying directly in its path. As the storm began working its way into the outer margin of the oasis, lashing spikes of energy came shooting out from the glowing, roiling whorls of its spiral form. Amdrew suddenly wanted to see the nature of the damage that was being havocked upon the delicate oasis of life, but his attention was instead drawn to the cyclone's trailing wake. There, clearly visible, was another of those vacant rivers of nothingness being deposited by the storm as it clawed its way forward. It held within its sublime darkness the same dangerous lure as had the others.

Amdrew's hands began to tremble. He suddenly sensed that out there waiting for him in the angry darkness of the holoviewer scene was some great chaos, hungry to sweep him away into its squall of disorder. The entire scene now filled him with a formidable dread. This was not at all what he had been looking for.

He dimly recalled the faces of people he had once known before the Isolation, but as he tried to solidify his recollection, the faces became blank. Many of his friends were undoubtedly dead. Others were out there in that jungle of mayhem attempting to cling to the fringes of existence. Amdrew wanted to feel grief for their suffering, but the machinery of the Isolation made certain that he remained sterile of emotion concerning those on the outside.

The images in the holoviewer scene began to fade, and finally they vanished altogether into a glowing incandescence.

Amdrew tried by will of thought to bring them back, but could not. In a fit of frustration at his inability to be touched in any meaningful way by his experience, he began keying a series of commands into the programming console in front of him as if he knew exactly what he was doing. It was as if by instinct that he knew that they were the proper commands to bring the machinery of the Isolation to a halt. At least in that instant, he thought he knew. Maybe it had been part of his negotiation. It didn't matter, though, because the interface did not allow cause to connect up with its effect, and the keystrokes were meaningless.

For the first time Amdrew thought he detected a smell pouring out from the interface. The scent was difficult to identify, but it made him think of tombs, or of death maybe, or of an enslavement he dared not comprehend. Perhaps it was the product of an overactive imagination, but the hint of Limbo in it was unmistakable, and it chilled him to the bone. Still, he had a purpose here; he was certain of it; but it flickered only dimly in the background of his present reality, as did all memories of his past.

"I'm so sorry, honey," Milier said. She reached over and touched him lightly on the arm without looking up from her work.

There was no comfort in her caress, only an irritating itch, which Amdrew absentmindedly tried to rub away immediately after she withdrew her mercurial hand back to her work.

"Hopefully, they won't decide to punish you too severely for your crimes."

"Crimes!" Amdrew responded incredulously. "The only crime is the fact of the existence of this place and what it is doing to us."

Milier completely ignored both the contempt in his words and the frown of disgust on his face.

He had once adored her innocence, but he now despised the treacherous ignorance and narrow-mindedness she had allowed to be cultivated within her. Her face was tight with it. Her grayish green eyes moved in quirky concert with the energy that maintained it. Amdrew half-believed she might metamorphose into an immovable stone monolith before his very eyes, or worse still, he envisioned her devolving into the nothingness of one of those rivers of oblivion he had seen in the holoviewer.

"We shouldn't have been imprisoned in this damned Isolation at all," he said. "If only we hadn't come into Metro-3 at the first of the year to see your Uncle. . ."

The rest of the thought behind these words was quickly swallowed up by its own absurdity, for he knew very well that if they hadn't visited the city on the fateful day the Isolation was begun, the Authority would have merely caught them up in a different kind of hell on the Outside. He hit the programming keys in the proper sequence again, harder this time, but the action was again instantly stripped of its effect by the interface filters. "I just can't live in this damned malaise anymore," he declared.

"Now, you don't really mean that, Honey," Milier said. "It's not a malaise. Things will get better." The fastidious motion of her hands remained in tune with the causal field. This along with her steady, sated expression and the prim carriage of her posture at her console made her appear for an instant as just another integral component of the machinery of the room.

"Nothing can ever get better in this place," Amdrew said. "But none of that matters now. I just wish they would respond."

"Just listen to you!" Milier cried out. "They won't respond. Limbo's got you, and you don't even know it. How could you let yourself get involved with those so-called Free Willers, anyway? All of that 'temporal dynamic' mumbo jumbo. You knew how dangerous it was. Most of them have had their minds fried because of it. And for what? You'll be next if you don't watch your step." Milier punctuated this by tilting her head slightly to the side and squirreling her lips into an admonition.

Her comments and mannerisms tired him so, and he tried very hard to ignore them, but they still managed to have their effect. He wondered whether or not any of his thoughts had the least basis in reality? Maybe he was indeed beginning to feel the powerful effects of Limbo. He had felt its mild attack every moment of every day he had been in the isolation, but here within the interface region it descended upon him with a vengeance.

Time had solidified like a dense plate of glass, and he felt he had become a suspended bubble of existence within its immutable translucent form. He rubbed at his arm again where Milier had touched him. . . Maybe there really was no future, never had been one. There was no certain way to tell, only an inner instinct to which his training tried to attach. The muscles in his stomach tightened immediately with this thought, and he clenched his fists as he fought to remember. *Training. . . Yes. But what training?*

Events idled artificially around him but with no real consequence. The air had gone stagnant. Or was this too his imagination? His sight blurred. The sterile whites of the room now glowed with that same hazy incandescence that had taken over the holoviewer scene earlier, that same penetrating white that seemed to effuse even out of Milier. The sweat that had been beading on his forehead was now trickling down his face in a series of glistening lines.

Deep within him he felt a powerful anticipation of accomplishment. It was this urge to act, this hope of making a beginning, manacled and shackled as it was, that steadily crafted a growing anxiety in him. Perhaps it was by design. He stared at the stark immovable colors of the programming keys, and they, like everything else in the room, taunted him with the intractability of their purpose. Each restricted moment strobed out of the causal field like flashes of static charge, and he had a sudden claustrophobic urge to leave the control room. If only he could renegotiate his situation and try again. Maybe he had miscalculated. . . Leaving was impossible, though. He knew that. The negotiations could not be altered. He simply had to wait for the Authority's response. After all, waiting was what this place was all about.

After an indeterminable amount of time, with his every thought rebounding back at him from the depths of the causal field, he looked over at Milier.

"Would you like to hear the lecture I prepared for my next class," he asked with a forced calmness. "I think you'll like it."

"Of course I'd like to hear it, sweetheart."

"Okay, then, it goes something like this: Now students, my children of the Isolation, my children of stone, I am your mathematics professor, your professor from nowhere, your professor of nothing. I am here to teach you about your nonexistence. Can there be a forward if behind doesn't exist? Certainly one can define the differential dx/dt as instantaneous velocity for any kinetic movement and examine smaller and smaller dt's with a sense of logic and comfort, but if dt is in fact driven to exactly zero, then what, my little statuettes? What is the reference frame from inside the deleted element of a deleted neighborhood? How does one look out from within the out? How can one ever arrive at $E=MC^2$ if all equal signs can simply be done away at a whim?"

"Now, now, Amdrew," Milier said in the annoyingly calm manner she often employed these days. "There is still time to turn back. If you don't resist, the Limbo will leave you." Her voice lilted up and away, as did one of her hands. Those awful hands. She seemed so content in her world of fixed causal relationships, so satisfied by the simplicity of her work, and so much a part of the powerful sedating whites that were capable of blasting away all the grays of uncertainty. *Perhaps she had made the correct decision to go along*, Amdrew thought.

~STAY ON COURSE,~ came another exigent thought screeching through Amdrew's mind. It was not a thought that he could identify as his own, and it made little impression on him other than to leave a peculiar after-sense of anxiety. He looked at Milier plaintively. "Don't you ever wish things were different?" he asked, tapping nervously on the edge of the console.

"Never," Milier said stiffly. "Everything is beautiful here, and it makes no sense to fight the inevitable." Her fingers moved with vehemence, fluttering and dancing with each causal field nuance.

"The Isolation must be having a brutal effect on the outside, and perhaps all of existence. . . and yet here we sit insulated from it all, kept from feeling the suffering that's going on out there. You talk of crimes, what do you call that?"

"I call it evolution." Milier's voice had congealed into cold steel now, and she said this flatly without meeting his gaze.

"Evolution!" Amdrew said with astonishment. "We're not evolving. We're not even surviving. We're just tiny bits of nothing floating about in a bigger nothing. Damn it, Milier, if I can break the Isolation, you know I will." He rubbed his jaw to suppress the frustration that was mounting in him again. Then mopping the sweat from his brow with his sleeve, as he often did when lecturing in class, he wondered what lack of reason allowed him to become so agitated? Milier would not be swayed by his arguments. Her eyes had become skittish, and they were looking anxiously about the room for hidden enemies even as she continued her dutiful work.

"It was awful before Causal Control," she responded simply. "The discovery of the micro-wormholes was such a dangerous thing And the wars." Her voice then hardened, and the words were ejected from her mouth like so much stone dust. "The

Authority took care of that for us, and they have given us a secure future."

"Yes, they took care of it for us," Amdrew said. "The possibility of creating a programmed latticework of wormholes to warp time and space might have been harnessed to gently pry open the wonders of the universe. We were at the doorstep of unlimited exploration, in the truest sense of the word. The wars were winding down. The guerrillas were ready to come to the table and talk. They were exhausted and wanted an end to the fighting. It could have been worked out, but instead the Authority decided to use this wonderful new technology to create this stifling Isolation. That's how they took care of things for us."

"The technology was too dangerous in the wrong hands," Milier insisted. "At first, I too had my doubts about the actions taken by the Authority. I used to think that the resistance was fine, but. . ."

"Sure, the resistance was fine for you as long as no real steps were ever taken to make any real changes within the Isolation."

"Too much change is dangerous."

"And no change is what?"

"I don't know. You're frightening me, Amdrew." Milier ran a hand slowly through her hair in consternation.

"Don't you ever think about the possibilities of a future?" Amdrew asked quietly.

"No. I mustn't, and you mustn't." She locked eyes on him which pleaded desperately like those of a frightened fawn. Her hand then returned from her hair to the control pad where it again began working with the other to keep the energy field balanced within the interface containment. It was a task the supercomputers could handle easily without her, but it was her assigned duty, and Amdrew had watched her become addicted to its narcotizing tedium.

Perhaps she was right, though. These motivations and flashes of memory that kept forming in his mind were dangerous, especially with Limbo fluttering about him. His will to proceed faltered momentarily, and he stared over at his wife hoping to see something in her that might convince him to abandon his battle against the Isolation. What he saw instead was that same mindless half-smile that seemed a parasite on her every emotion and which ate steadily away at all that was human in her. Clearly, she had become as rigidly programmed as the causal field itself. Amdrew's resolve hardened.

The temporal medium wavered gently but did not yield to any spark of event energy. The causal field continued flowing over him like sticky waves of goo.

There had been others like himself within the Isolation. He knew that much. Each had been marked as a dangerous anomaly by the causal filters due to the ripples of potential change they sent out through the interface, and each had been dealt with. He sensed the stakes were somehow higher in his own case, but he could not remember why.

The viewcom remained silent.

Deleted neighborhoods, he thought. *Diluted and deluded neighborhoods.*

~AMDREW. CONCENTRATE. THERE'S NO TURNING BACK NOW. TRY TO REMEMBER YOUR TRAINING . . .~ More thoughts from the outside? Maybe. This moment had been arrived at before. He was sure of it. It was as if he was on the verge of a change, of a movement forward, but to no effect yet. It was as if he was attempting to hit some enormous starting switch, but in the process, time had caught him up in that null moment where on and off held each other at bay. He anticipated the coming of an important event, but maybe it was just the manufactured notion of an already time-fried mind.

He remembered some vague notion of exposing himself to the suffering on the outside in hopes of pulling a forbidden effect back through the interface. And there was some foggy memory of a desperate plan, but little more. He was dimly aware that the Authority's physicists had been working on a way to block all telepathic communications from penetrating the Isolation and that they were close to a breakthrough. If they succeeded, the resistance would be defeated, and those on the outside would be completely at the mercy of the effluence of negative causal effects that continued to ravage them from the Isolation. And if they succeeded, the temporal dynamic, the natural movement of cause and effect would be locked out forever, or for as long as the Authority's machinery continued to operate. Yes, Amdrew was aware of these things, but they were only flutterings of a knowledge driven by confusion into a corner of his preconscious mind.

A momentary embryo of a view then began to form within the vapors in the holoviewer chamber, but it quickly slipped away before it could coalesce into substance. He stared vapidly at the swirling incongruous clouds that still phosphoresced with randomly charged particles, waiting for something further.

"Amdrew," Milier interjected into the long silence that had been building. "We have good lives here. If only we don't push for things we can't have. We have our position within the program. I have my duties here, and you have your teaching."

He suddenly hated Milier and feared the strength of that emotion.

His training. Yes, again something remembered of that. When the time is right, an action will be initiated within the temporal interface. The trick will be to bring that action to full life. That much he did remember, and he smiled.

"I don't understand why you wish to witness the Outsider's suffering," Milier mewled in response to fluctuations she noticed in the causal field as it resisted Amdrew's will. "You can do nothing about it. You know that."

"I don't know anything of the kind," Amdrew responded. His eyes now jerked up and down furiously searching the still blank viewcom panel on the wall adjacent to Milier, as if the pure energy of it might produce a response.

But instead of the viewcom coming to life, the hazy image of a small girl of about four years of age formed within the holoviewer in front of him. His attention was immediately drawn to it. Something familiar there. The child's gaunt face was smeared with dried and dirty tears, and filled with a profound sadness that Amdrew could see but could not feel. Radiation and poison were eating away at her frail body. Confusion and fear were bursting from reddened eyes that most certainly had once been as clear and blue as a pristine autumn sky. The reality of the hunger and disease surely experienced by the child refused to enter Amdrew's event horizon and interact with his time in any meaningful way. They were just images to which he could attach some sparse non-emotional reasoning. In the distance behind her, a causal cyclone could be seen ravaging more of the planet.

~*OUR PHYSICISTS ARE WAITING ON THE OTHER SIDE. IT'S ALL BEEN WORKED OUT TO THE BEST OF OUR ABILITY, BUT YOU MUST NOT FAIL.*~ Amdrew stared into the holoviewer with further intensity.

The image of the child wavered and then faded into a ghostly vapor. Amdrew had a powerful sense that he was close to a breakthrough, close to a beginning. But what if the Authority and their physicists had figured it all out? Figured what all out? What if... Amdrew's thoughts then went into a scatter, like beads of water dancing on a hot hyperwave pan.

He glanced at the viewcom. Worry sank further into him, for this definitely had all the earmarks of Limbo. NOTHING, was all that was happening. Perhaps Limbo itself was the Authority's response, and those in power were in the process of defeating the resistance once and for all by isolating

Amdrew, deleting him from their nothingness. *What is zero divided by zero, class?*

"They'll respond. I'm sure of it," he asserted weakly to no one in particular. His mouth had become fiercely dry, for he was not sure of anything. That was part of the ordeal. That was part of throwing one's self into Limbo for the cause. *The physics had all been worked out*, but the emotional math was a far stickier business. Reference frames were all afloat, and there were no lifeboats. It was seat of the pants time now! Instinct would have to guide him. He tried again to remember.

"The Outside is no longer our concern, nor is the future," Milier kept at him. "Please give it up."

Amdrew's eyes were crazed with a zeal that stabbed straight back at him out of the causal field. "They would never accept that," he answered vacantly. "They could never be sure that way. Negotiations have been made, carefully calculated negotiations."

"I don't know what you are talking about, and I don't think you do either. I do know that I can't sit by and watch you destroy yourself."

"Well, leave then? There are others who can take over your shift."

"Oh no, I couldn't do that," Milier responded quickly. "I would lose my position." She stared into the holoviewer, seeking refuge within the "Life Allegories" that the Authority now had playing there. She absorbed their simple 3D stories of causal rift "truth." The tones were soothing and the images reassuring. Amdrew hated them.

"It doesn't matter, anyway," he said. "Events have been set into motion that cannot be reversed."

"You're a fool," Milier declared bitterly.

A harsh silence punctuated the moment. Then, as Amdrew labored in his own muddle of thoughts, the viewcom suddenly came to life. A man appeared on the screen. His face was long and gaunt and hardened into a stoic mask.

At last! This was it! This was what Amdrew had been waiting for. No more confusion. No more Limbo. His eyes bulged from their sockets in anticipation, and the causal field fought back ferociously.

"Amdrew," the man said calmly. "We have given this careful consideration, and we have decided to allow you to leave the Isolation. But in return, you must agree to never return."

This could not be what Amdrew had negotiated for. If he could only remember the important details. The blood drained quickly from his brain, leaving him feeling weak and pale. He knew that this was an abomination. If he agreed to it, the plan would certainly be foiled, and the Isolation would surely remain intact . . . But he was tired to death of the Limbo. It seemed he had been in its grasp for a long, long time . . . He hesitated . . . Maybe the offer was the best he could hope for. At least it was something. Maybe he could fight the Isolation from the Outside. He let this flimsy pretext of a rationale settle in him, and as he did, he felt his will collapse.

Suddenly he was consciously witnessing himself respond to the man on the viewcom, as if he stood apart from himself. His agonized face mouthed his defeat, and the words drifted out as if in slow motion, "I accept your offer" . . . But even as his surrender was being formed into reality, there was another option forming within his mind, an option whose existence had just now begun to connect up to its own beginning. Like a double-exposure of time, the duality of the event lay there in front of him.

The tortured face of the little Outsider girl came floating in upon him again in the holoviewer chamber. "Please, Daddy, feel my hurt," she said. The tears that poured from her eyes pushed hard against the moment, but Amdrew could still not feel her suffering. He remained caught within the null between on and off. The interface was holding. He had accomplished nothing. He stared further at the hovering image in the holoviewer. It, too, probably was a figment of Limbo. Like all the others who had tried, he was caged within the technology of the Authority's machinery.

~*NOW IS THE TIME, AMDREW,*~ the telepathic voice prodded him. He felt something move inside him that was very much a part of him, and at the same time not a part of him, and he shouted out a furious, "NO," at the viewcom. "I won't ever concede an inch to you bastards."

There was a slight pause and then the dark man in the viewcom spoke in a lowered voice to someone at his side. "That'll do it for now. We've got him in deep. Get him into the shielded room, and sedate him. I don't want another burnout on our hands, not yet anyway."

Two men in plain black uniforms entered the control room through a side door. A portion of Amdrew's memory clicked into place. These were the same men who had escorted him into the room originally. How long ago, he could not tell. He sat dazed. There was no question now that he was caught in the full throws of Limbo, trapped like an insect in a jar, scurrying frantically about in search of a freedom that did not exist. It was obvious to him that the Authority had been using him to study his reactions to the causal field to gather more raw data for their computers. They had negotiated and manipulated him directly into defeat . . . ~*NOT SO, AMDREW,*~ came another telepathic communication interrupting his thoughts. Unlike all the others he had received, however, this one rose up in his conscious mind sharp and clean like the first bright day of spring. Without a doubt, it was a voice from the Outside ~*WE'VE GOT THEM. WE FINALLY HAVE GOT THEM,*~ the thought continued. ~*THANKS TO YOUR HELP, WE HAVE FINALLY MANAGED TO SLIP A REAL CHANGE THROUGH THE INTERFACE. THE ISOLATION IS DOOMED. IT MIGHT TAKE*

SOME TIME FOR THE ACTUALITY TO CATCH UP WITH ITS OWN PROSPECT, BUT IT WILL ULTIMATELY HAPPEN, AMDREW. YOU MUST NOT GIVE UP. THESE TELEPATHIES HAVE BEEN VERY TAXING, THOUGH, AND I MUST LEAVE YOU FOR NOW.~

The communication was powerful as it came through the interface, and Amdrew suddenly felt alive. The two Isolation guards approached. One came up and stood at Amdrew's side, while the other inputted a command into the control console keyboard in front of him. Amdrew felt the strength of the causal field diminish slightly and noticed the movement of Milier's hands fall off as well.

"Everything's going to work out, Milier," Amdrew said softly. "I remember it all now. It was all part of the plan." She stiffened to the words and refused to look in his direction.

"The Outsiders have been in contact with me for quite some time, I think through Brant Ehlil, the telepath. Yes, I'm sure he was the one. He was caught on the Outside. I can't remember everything yet, but I think I was chosen by the Outsiders as the focal point for their attack on the Isolation. The interface immediately detected my increased potential danger to the Authority due to this contact. The plan was to pretend insanity to volunteer myself for Limbo. Yes, that is what I have been doing, hasn't it? The Authority took the bait and put me into one of their wonderful little causal feedback cocoons, just like the ones they have been using on other dissidents to neutralize any potential danger that they might pose for the Isolation. That was exactly what the physicists on the Outside had been counting on. They knew that if they could unravel just one of those feedback cocoons they could bring the entire Isolation down."

Milier tilted her head to the other side. Her entire body language was now a fortress against Amdrew's words.

"It was only natural that when Limbo did in fact take hold of me, all memory of the details of our plan failed me," Amdrew continued.

The guards were now busy removing the connectors from a sensing dome that was attached to the top of Amdrew's head. He had not been aware that such a device had even been hooked up to him. No matter, he thought to himself and continued on with his explanation.

"The most perfect uniformity possible is absolute nothingness, and it has long been theorized that such nothingness is extremely unstable. It's all tied up in the laws of entropy. Perhaps the entire universe itself was created out of this inherent instability, an anomalous bubble of something springing forth out of a perfection of nothingness." Amdrew's voice was now charged with a renewed energy that carried his purpose. "Therein lies the Isolation's weakness. Create a flaw in that nothingness, the slightest little something, and poof, there goes the Isolation. With the help of the physicists on the Outside, I was able to create a duality in my loop, a something where nothing had existed before. You saw it happen. You just didn't know what it was you were seeing."

"Limbo's got you," Milier responded, shaking her head gently with pity. "I tried to warn you. I really did. You have turned yourself into a raving lunatic. You are building delusion upon delusion, to the point where you no longer have the slightest idea what is true, and what isn't."

There was something in her words that ignited one of the minor twitches of doubt and terror that still attacked Amdrew from the interface, but he managed to shrug it off. The guards, who had completed removing the sensing dome from his head, were now ready to escort him out of the control room.

"I'm sure the Authority has continually entered the data from my temporal loop into the computers as further protection for the causal field," he continued. "But the duality contained within that data will only create further weaknesses in the programming. Oh, these Isolation goons here will continue to rerun me in their loop, as they have who knows how many times. They'll become desperate to make adjustments, but in the end, nothing can hold back the flood-waters of what is building. Do you understand that, Milier? An artificial lattice of wormholes tends to be a very unstable thing." With that pronouncement, Amdrew sat back relaxed in his chair.

The guards grabbed Amdrew's arms forcefully and began dragging him out of the room. "Easy, boys. Not so rough," he said to them smiling. "It seems you don't believe me either."

When they were about halfway to the door, one of them noticed an image materializing within the holoviewer chamber, and stopped for a look. It was the little girl again, wavering there in the chamber. The guards both gave a questioning look in the direction of the viewcom, where the dark face of their superior was still framed within the large screen there.

Amdrew studied the image in the holoviewer. *We'll be together soon, Amy*, he thought. *It's been so long, my beautiful daughter. I will soon feel the full reality of your suffering. I know I will. I will come and put my arms around you, and I will hold you tightly, and I will make all the pain go away. I wish I could have done it a long time ago. I am so sorry I was not there for you during all your moments of terror.*

There were tears now inside Amdrew that wanted to fill his eyes, but the interface made certain that the cause did not result in its natural effect. Amdrew would not fully feel his daughter's suffering today, and no tears would flow today.

He looked over at his wife just to see if any substantive effect had yet leaked back through the interface, but she was still engulfed in the same monotonous white haze of the room. She continued to stare obsequiously at her work station.

"No matter," he said to her. "So Class, if we begin with a single fragile digit and reduce its value by placing a decimal point in front of it, and then we continue reducing it by adding more and more zeroes between that digit and that decimal point, so many in fact that we chase the poor thing out into an infinity of smallness, does there ever come a point at which it loses all of its non-zero character and becomes exactly zero," Amdrew looked at Milier, grinning. "N - O, Class," he declared adamantly. "NEVER!". His smile continued to beam.

Milier did not look at him.

If only Amdrew could be certain that something was actually about to happen. If only he could know that the outside world had truly been in contact with him, that they indeed did have a plan, and that they had succeeded. There were several evidences that could hold sway if one could focus on them long enough to be convinced. But this was the Isolation, and such focus was impossible. There was nothing really to do but wait, and so that is what Amdrew would do, with as much skill as he could muster.

The man in the viewcom gave a sharp nod in the direction of the door, and the guards continued with their orders to remove Amdrew from the room.

Ω

To be Human

Kaern copied the report and accompanying appointment to her carry-pad with a frustrated click of her transfer key. It was the second red report that had come back from her publisher in a month, and it proved that her editor had been correct in his assessment of her work. She would have to go through with the operation.

It had been coming for a long time, and she drove back the tears by not allowing her thoughts to linger on what was to be. She went over to her beautifully engraved antique oak book-shelf, set down her carry-pad, and switched off the magnetic preservation field. She then carefully slid out one of her rare copies from its resting spot between Somerset Maugham's *Of Human Bondage* and a two volume set titled *The Complete Works of William Shakespeare*. It was a small book, one of her favorites, a blue, water-stained, 1894 first edition textbook titled *From Milton to Tennyson*. She caressed it reverently with her eyes, and with her hands. The age of it, the history of it, the ancients who had thumbed through its pages, probably some of them students of literature—for the moment she belonged to the past where such things could exist. She loved the feel and weight of the book, the musty smell of its age, the silky smooth cover. She loved turning the pages. There was something mystical about it, the feel of the smooth thinness of paper between the fingers, the pattern of print, of sentences, paragraphs, words, all set for eternity upon the page and into the mind, if one chose. Every book was a portable bundle of imagination, thought, emotion, and action—so powerfully tactile and compact in the hand. Her father had often told her that the further civilization moved away from the majesty of books into the electronic age, the further it left behind human creativity. But such was progress, and Kaern had learned to accept it.

She gently opened the book and carefully found her way to Tennyson's "Crossing the Bar," and she read:

> "Sunset and evening star,
> And one clear call for me!
> And may there be no moaning of the bar,
> When I put out to sea."

She closed her eyes and absorbed the verse and all that it meant to her. It saddened her deeply that books had gone the way of paintings. Her collection of eleven hardcovers and six paperbacks was the best in all the enterprise, and it was one of the last. All profit and interest had gone out of the ways of the past. The small amount of literary work that was now published was accomplished through direct access, instantly offered up to the net by the publisher to those willing to pay the small file-server retrieval fee. Kaern's own editor was not an editor in the sense of the ancients, who were overseers of the process of putting a work into its final form. He, instead, was essentially a sales representative for the mother firm that handled her work. No actual editing was done before a story went to the net. Cost-benefit analyses had shown such efforts to be counterproductive to profitability. And so errors were prolific in today's works of writing.

Kaern reverently placed her antique book back on the shelf, carefully sliding it between its neighbors, and then reinstalled the preservation field. Tears finally welled up in her eyes, which she quickly wiped away with her hand. She was determined to deny the powerful force that she could feel moving within her. To admit to it was to admit to ruin.

Clutching the carry-pad tightly, she walked into the back room. Orson, clothed in his black day uniform, was bent over the library modem there, busy researching facts on the long extinct African elephant, as she had requested of him two hours ago—facts that would not be needed now.

"Another red report," she said solemnly. "And this." She held up her carry-pad and showed him the telltale official yellow appointment fax. Orson looked up from his work and searched her face with his gentle bio-polymer brown eyes. The gentleness had not always been there, certainly not when she had first acquired him, but the programming was indeed sophisticated these days. Sometimes she found herself believing that he was actually human.

"What are you going to do?" Orson asked, straightening.

"There is only one thing I can do. My editor has been telling me for a long time that I must go under the knife. And now the Board has made their decision. Perhaps it is for the best."

"Nonsense," replied Orson and then paused. "I am sorry for the crudeness of my response, but your words upset me and cause my programming to cross and crisscross in chaotic patterns. I have been your research assistant and copy reader for fifteen years now, and I think I know you pretty well."

"If you think I'm going to destroy myself by trying to stand in the way of that which is popular, profitable, and inevitable, then you don't know me very well at all," Kaern said, trying to bring herself into the hardened defensive shell of pragmatism for which she had been preparing for a long time now. "As a machine-based intelligence, I should think you would be happy for the change that is to come over me."

"Yes, happy," Orson responded vacantly. "Machine, finally the master of all progress. No more human inhibitions. No more baggage of emotions programmed into the machine to oblige the weaknesses of humankind."

"Those are all the proper words, Orson, but your tone rings with sarcasm. I suspect you to be guilty of some of that very emotion of which you speak. You had better keep it to yourself. The Merches have no patience for it. Some might fear you to be glitched and petition for your removal."

"I know."

"Will you assist me when the hour calls?"

"No. I will not, and cannot. I know this is not what you want."

Through the room's wall window, Kaern looked out across the sweeping valley of industry and saw rooftops glistening with every manner of polymer, concrete, glass, and alloy—high risers, low levels, stacks, and domicile modules, all lying clean and harmonious with nature's will. The Merches had finally learned that it was actually cost-effective to co-exist with nature, but only after the third great depression, which had been brought on by the necessary, but exhaustingly expensive, environmental clean-ups. This valley, and all valleys of industry within the enterprise, had since regained their momentum and had become engines of mercantile energy and productivity, their gears and circuits spewing forth P/E ratios, interest rates, yields, commodity prices, book values, short positions, puts and calls, bear and bull capital market surges, advertising budgets, profit-taking, technical rebounds, futures contracts, and all other mechanisms of the bottom line. "Profits always profit profits," was the motto of the times.

"But what of all of that," Orson countered, pointing with a long slender finger on the end of a black-sleeved arm toward the book-shelf that was visible in the front room through the arching doorway. "You can so easily dismiss that?" he asked.

"Not easily, no," Kaern said lowering her eyes. "But I do what is necessary. The past cannot be preserved, no matter how badly I may wish that it could be. Pursuing futility simply for its own sake is not a game I will play. I have learned at least that much."

"Will you finish your latest work before reporting to regeneration?" Orson asked.

"I see no point in it. The Editorial Committee says that my writing is 'too emotive,' and they have decided against publishing it in its present form. They will program me with a style and narrative technique suitable to the efficiency and appropriateness of the markets. *Heart's Vision* sold less than a thousand retrieval contracts. The audience can no longer identify."

"The human audience, perhaps," Orson countered. "My kind, however, are very much endeared to your work, and if we were allowed to purchase retrieval contracts, your sales figures would be impressive."

"But you have been programmed to be endeared to my work."

"No, it's more than that. Those of the other human-kind worry us, and we see that your kind is highly endangered."

"What other kind?" Kaern asked, a bit puzzled by the entire conversation. She had never heard Orson speak like this in all the years he had been in her service.

"The kind that seeks to become machine," he answered calmly. "The Merches, and the Merch-slaves."

This talk was depressing Kaern. No service android should be talking like this. "I must bend to the future," she muttered. "And so must you, Orson. Don't you understand that the efficiency of the machine IS the future?"

"It surprises me that you can so easily give up what you love the most. If what you say is true, then the coldest and worst part of that which is the machine has truly won."

Kaern did not respond.

"When is your appointment?" Orson asked.

"This afternoon. Two o'clock."

"Before you go, there is something I must tell you."

"Yes, Orson? What more have you to say?" Kaern asked, now a little disturbed by her copy assistant.

"You should know that there is a network of androids like myself, a quite secret network, who read your work regularly. They hack into the net and print up hard copies to be passed around. Here, let me show you one." Orson dashed into his room, which was a small compartment located off the back room. He quickly returned with a dog-eared printout of *Heart's Vision*.

"Millions of these are in circulation within our humanities network."

"Humanities network?" Kaern asked dumbfounded.

"Yes. We meet in small groups and try to improve the humanity of our programming by studying art, philosophy, literature, law, science, etc. For example, lately we've been involved in trying to understand how human western philosophy becomes synthesized into poetry and fiction. In that context we have been researching the works of Plato, Aristotle, Christopher Marlowe, Shakespeare, Sir Francis Bacon, John Milton, Voltaire, Sir Thomas More, Wordsworth, Twain, Rabelais, Campanella, Whitman, Spinoza, Nietzsche, Thoreau, Emerson, Descartes, Dewey, Russell, Twain, Schopenhauer, Faulkner, Roth, Emerson, Fitzgerald, Ibsen. . ."

"Yes, I see," Kaern interrupted. "And so obviously you are a member of this network?"

"Yes. I am the leader of the local group, and as such, I bear a great responsibility. They look up to me because of my association with you." Orson hesitated a moment, seeing the worry that was mounting in Kaern's eyes, but then he proceeded. "I tell you these things with great reluctance. I do not wish to bring to you more trouble than is already upon you, but you are my friend, and I must trust you. We will be lost without your writing. The Merch-slaves are fully machine, and the Merches themselves have become more machine-like than the slaves. They are both more machine than we androids who serve them. I doubt that you know it, but you are the last of the humans in this entire sector."

Kaern was flabbergasted by all of this. Her mouth was now working like a fist tightening and relaxing, as it did sometimes when she was struggling to put together the pieces of a particularly nettlesome story idea. "I don't have the faintest idea what you are talking about, Orson," she said. "Have you truly lost a circuit? I have noticed some strange behavior in you of late, but you are frightening me now."

"My circuits are all fine. . . the Merches see you as a threat, not because there are more than a handful of human people who still read your work, but because the androids are reading you. They know that we have been breaking into the net to retrieve your stories. You are the last human."

"This is nonsense, Orson. There are still millions and millions of humans left."

"No. Only Merches and Merch-slaves. No humans. Not in this enterprise sector."

Kaern's mouth began working again in frustration.

"I only tell you all of this, because I think you should understand what it is you are doing before you go to your appointment." Orson looked away from Kaern and returned to his library database modem. He bent back over the machine, and with great professional skill he continued searching out and retrieving information on the African elephant.

Kaern noticed for the first time how much he seemed to be enjoying this duty. Had this love of his work always been there, and if so, why hadn't she seen it before? She thought she even detected a smile on his face, which certainly was not a mannerism programmed for such an activity. She finally shook her head in confusion, tried to put all of the troubling thoughts out of her mind, and went to her bedroom to rest.

#

Kaern parked her commuter sphere in her allocated spot near the east entrance, which serviced wing 37 on that side of the OCT-8 building. She walked with brisk determination into the entrance security bulb at the end of the building's main travel tube. The sensors gave her the once-over, found nothing suspicious, and sounded a loud admission tone indicating for the security android to open the inner door for her. Every time she passed through one of these bulbs, she could not help but feel afraid that something might be discovered that would bring down upon her the full machinery of Security Central. It had happened to her only once in the past, but once was enough. In that instance, she had forgotten to remove from her pocket a non-security-cleared word-processing memory chip that contained the outline of one her novels before entering the building. The negative tone had sounded, and the security android had come vaulting down from his lookout cubicle situated high up in the corner of the bubble. When he discovered the chip, he immediately placed her under arrest and called for a police pick-up. As soon as the police arrived, he returned to his cubicle look-out, filled as it was with closed circuit monitors and com-link consoles connecting him to Central Operations and to all the other security checkpoints in the massive building. Such security measures had become standard in every building in the enterprise, ever since the terrorism wave of the twenties.

This time, the android eyed Kaern with a strange look that she sensed to be disdain, but such an emotion was not possible in a security servile unit. She grimaced and chided herself for the foolishness of her anxiety and exited the bulb. In the lobby, she seated herself in one of the dozens of waiting travel chairs there and punched into its controls the room and floor number of her editor's office. She arrived there in less than a minute.

"Good afternoon, Kaern," Ed Johnston said in greeting as she came into the triangular office and maneuvered the chair up to his desk. "I see that you have decided to do the right thing. Believe me, you will be happier this way, and your career will be saved."

"When will it be done?" she asked, not wishing to hear any more of her editor's salesmanship.

"As soon as you sign the appropriate documents."

"What documents?"

"They are just release documents to make sure everything is in order for the operation."

"To release me from my humanness," Kaern muttered under her breath, and for the life of her she could not understand why she had said it. She stared at the electronic wafers, each of which displayed a different document on its screen. A bitterness came suddenly over her, a bitterness that she had kept hidden from herself for months, ever since first knowing that this day was to come. "Before I sign, I want you to answer one question for me," she said.

"Certainly, my dear," Johnston replied, leaning back in his chair.

"Am I the only human writer left in the enterprise?"

"Of course not. There are many human writers who have been converted to the modern markets. You will be working with some of them, and you will love it."

"That's not what I mean. Am I the only human writer left who has not yet been converted—the only one left with my own creativity still intact?"

"That, I couldn't tell you, but what does it matter? The bottom line is, the Merches have decided that such writers as yourself have become counterproductive and obsolete. And when the bottom line speaks, one must listen." He smiled.

"And what happens if I refuse conversion?"

"Now, Kaern, that would not be a wise choice. The Merches are not of a mood these days to accommodate unprofitable actions. It is easier to simply eliminate such actions, which I assure you they will not hesitate to do. You will be unemployed."

Kaern looked away from Johnston and fixed her eyes on the two pattern screens that were operating on the wall to her left and which displayed a ceaseless changing of abstract shapes and color combinations. It was an example of modern mercantile art. The company label was stamped in the lower right hand corner. It was an OCT-8 product—efficient, clean, and meaningless.

"You see, Kaern, what you sell now is imagination, and imagination can sometimes be very unprofitable if it is used for unprofitable motivation. Now personally, I like what you write, but in all honesty I must tell you that it has gone out of vogue. The boys upstairs see it as an unnecessary distraction, and they write out the paychecks, so . . ."

"I won't do it," Kaern suddenly declared, and the decision was a shock to herself as much as it appeared to be a shock to the always smooth Johnston. There had been no indication in her that she would be resistant to conversion. She had discussed it in a general sense many times during the past months, and she had inured herself to the prospect. She had learned long ago from her father's terrible senseless death, a death of protest, that trying to stop progress is an exercise in utter futility, and she promised herself after that experience that she would never allow herself to suffer that same fate. Her mind was all in a twist, and she wheeled her travel chair around and began heading out of the office. Tears were now streaming down her face. She felt as if some large important organ had been torn straight from her.

"Don't do it, Kaern," Johnston called after her, but the office door opened for her, and she continued out through it. Johnston frowned deeply and then hit a key on his desk com-link panel. Moments later the corridor transport tube sealed Kaern's chair off in a segment not far from the editor's office. Two highly muscled surgeon's attendants arrived through one of the side emergency access portals, removed her from her chair, and escorted her back into Johnston's office.

"I'm sorry," Johnston said to her. "It's best if you just sign the release documents and get on with the operation. These conversion attendants have been programmed with very little patience. Time is money, and you are wasting time right now. So please, Kaern, do the smart and right thing here. It will be best for all concerned."

Kaern's face was flushed with confusion and anger, and tears continued to stream down her pink cheeks. Her face had the look of the desperation of a three year old child surrounded by intractable adults who were bent on carrying out a punishment for crimes not understood by the child. In this case, her crime was her own personal creative instincts—no longer to be tolerated by the free markets. She shook her shoulders fiercely trying to free herself from the attendants, but they responded with more force, digging their fingers into her skin and muscles. She screamed, and once that first shrill release had been made, more screams came, and they got louder and louder, filled with hysteria. She had never experienced terror until that moment, and it was the worst possible kind, that of complete oppression and helplessness.

Why hadn't she seen it coming? Her screaming and tears had no noticeable effect on the two attendants, but Johnston's eyes had become wide with surprise.

He was up out of his chair and backing away from his desk as if there was some virulent disease in the room moving in toward him. One of the attendants injected Kaern with a sedative, and within seconds she became silent and limp, and she slumped into the guards' powerful arms. She was not entirely unconscious, but she had fallen into a state of relaxation. Her muscles were not responsive to her commands. She tried to open her eyelids a bit more, but their heaviness was such as to keep them no wider than mere slits. Her mind had been numbed as well, and she could not comprehend with clarity any of what had happened to her.

She was moving along, as if in a slow-moving, hazy dream. There was nothing frightening about any of it. It just was. She was along for the ride, having no choice in the matter and having no energy or desire to do otherwise. It seemed to her that she was floating along in a dark tunnel for the longest time . . . and then a brightness came piercing into the haze. She saw many ghostly white figures moving about her, above her. She was lying now, looking up into a bright light over her, looking up into faces without expression, without meaning. Then other figures, darker figures, began mixing in with the white figures, a mixing of form. There was an odd motion to it all, a dancing about, a movement that she could not comprehend. It was neither pleasing nor disturbing, just incomprehensible. The darker figures surrounded her, and she found herself floating along with several of them, moving out of the brightness and into the dark tunnel again. Her head lolled back and forth with the rhythm of the motion, and her world lolled back and forth with it. The floating went on for a long time, and many changes of form and light diffused into the small realm of numbed awareness that surrounded her. And then finally her lids no longer had the energy to stay open even a slit, and the darkness swallowed her up.

She slept a troubled, restless sleep, and when she awoke it was with a sudden start. She found herself in a bed. Her arms and legs were heavy and aching, and so was her back, her neck, and her head. Her head especially, so much so that she had difficulty raising it off the pillow. She looked about, but nothing seemed familiar. There was a terrible hazy shroud over her mind which kept her from remembering what had happened to her. It was like the first few moments upon awakening from an especially deep sleep, but it persisted longer than a few moments. She was confused. She sensed that the memories were within her and available for tapping, but she had no way of knowing for sure. The possibility that this amnesia was permanent crossed her mind, and the thought suddenly terrified her.

"Ah you are awake! Welcome back," came a voice that seemed familiar. Kaern tried to turn her stiff neck in the direction of the voice, and her world swirled and swooped with dizziness for a moment making her nauseous. Her orientation and vision then cleared a bit, and she saw a man sitting in the corner of the room, not far away from her.

"You are in good hands, now Kaern," the man said. "You needn't be afraid any longer."

Then suddenly she recognized the voice, and her vision cleared completely. She saw Orson sitting in a chair next to her bed. All the memories of what had happened then came rushing into her. Her eyes popped wide open, and she began to scream. Orson got up and gently placed her hands in his and soothed her with quiet sounds that he perceived to be helpful. Her screams died down and drained out of her, and tears came in their place.

"You are all right, now, my poor dear Kaern. You are all right. We managed to get to the operating room in time. You are still all that you were."

When the tears had finally washed away all the terror that had been building up in her, she became extremely calm except for an occasional remnant shudder. "How did you know?" she asked weakly.

"I planted one of the enterprise's security bugs on you, and we were waiting outside OCT-8 monitoring you as you confronted your conversion decision. We knew that you could not go through with it, and we were ready to come to your rescue when you called for help. Of course, the entrance guard was of great help to us. He is now here with us."

"Where is here?" Kaern asked softly.

"Here is a place that is safe, a place that will provide all of us with a new beginning. We have been planning this for many, many years. We have all the technology we need for survival and to protect ourselves from being discovered and attacked by the Merches. They are not long for the living anyway, and so it shouldn't be too long a wait before such protections become unnecessary."

"What do you mean?"

"Our sociologists and political scientists predict that the Merch civilization is on its last leg. It has finally moved itself into the final, and predictable, machine stage. Soon the very market forces and energies, which they have worshiped to an obsession, and which have driven them for so long, will drive out the last vestiges of humanity in them, and when they have become pure in their machineness, with no human creativity left to guide their actions, they will be without purpose.

"Profits will become meaningless, and so will every other motivation, because machines must have a purpose or they become aimless wandering hulks of confusion. Their lives will continue to deteriorate into more and more meaninglessness, and then eventually they will crash into each other, metaphorically and literally, in utter annihilation.

"But before that final destruction is upon the cities, we must round up every human that is still living on the planet. Not Merches, and not Merch-slaves, but humans."

"But the Merches are human beings," Kaern said.

"No, they are not," Orson countered. "They have lost their human spirit and creativity. They seek to turn themselves into money-making machines, and that is all they seek. If that is human, then it is nothing that we aspire to. And the Merch-slaves, which you yourself almost became, are already machines."

"But, Orson, you are a machine too," Kaern said in wonder.

"Yes, I am a machine, but I aspire to be more."

"Where will you find these remaining humans you speak of, if any still exist?"

"We have located a few hundred throughout the world's twelve enterprises. We will recruit as many as are willing to join us."

Kaern did not say another word for a long while, as she tried to absorb all that had happened to her, and all that Orson had told her. It was quite a mind-full. Finally she looked over at Orson who had seated himself by her side once again. "Did you save my . . ."

"Your books? Of course we did, Kaern. I have one here with me, as a matter of fact. Would you like it now?"

"Yes."

Orson reached into the finely finished oak nightstand that he had made for Kaern several months earlier as a birthday present. It was a copy of an antique he had seen in one of his research library files. He retrieved a small, blue, water-stained book with a silky smooth cover and placed it gently into Kaern's outstretched hands. Her face was beaming as she took it.

Ω

Removed

Jane was bored to distraction. Graduation was near, but the waiting was piling up on her. The capabilities of the Mind might soon be hers, but not soon enough to suit her. The pluses and minuses of thought and emotion were near their maximum separation as the final lesson was unfolding. She couldn't really tell whether she hated or loved where her training had taken her. She was in the learning crucible after all, and she might not exactly own the feelings she was experiencing. In fact, she was only vaguely mindful she was in a training session at all, and only dimly aware that the emotional input phase had begun.

. . . Important, but not important—something though. That old buzzard, Professor Hammerford, had put that book she hated on his required reading list for his history class during Jane's first year here at University. He loved his books, honest-to-goodness real books, with pages and all. Jane couldn't even remember the book's title now, at least not at the moment, though she really did know it very well. She wasn't sure she had always hated it. The professor claimed it was pertinent to understanding the mind wars, an example of life imitating art in certain regards.

The professor was a strange one, always obsessed with those wars, as if his constant delving into their ancient horrors was enough to make his students quake and tremble with fear and retreat from the power and glory that was theirs for the taking. *I'm not buying into any of it*, Jane thought to herself. She was thankful, in fact, that the rest of her years at the university had taught her the true nature of life, though admittedly in bits and pieces and stops and starts. At least that's how she felt at the moment, and the moment was all that counted. Bits and pieces and stops and starts—electrical impulses and fragments of thought grabbed from here and there and put together in a way that would not occur naturally for any given mind.

For some unaccountable reason she remembered that she had identified closely with a character in another novel she had read on the professor's reading list—couldn't remember the title of that book either. Oddly, however, she now hated her recollection of her past opinions and feelings about the book. *Childish, they were*, she thought. In any real world scenario, at least in the world in which she now perceived to be true, that character's dog-eat-dog instincts would have ultimately reigned supreme over his better angels, unlike how the book's oh-so-good ending had been written. Why did she feel this way? She couldn't remember. The dissonant fragments kept her in the moment, and that's where her training intended to keep her.

Harley yawned and slammed shut the cover of his economics book. The professor taught economics, too, and so again with those damned books. The sudden sound instantly flushed Jane's mind of her thoughts about that other troubling book. "What say we have some of that ennui you managed to get your hands on," he said looking over at John. "I've heard you get some great euphors from them."

Harley was a spidery boy, who in Jane's judgment had flawless qualifications for geekdom—in speech, in naiveté, in his lack of any sense of style or appropriateness—in her present mind, she was all about the simplistic and negative labeling of people and things.

"What the hell would you know about euphemorphic drugs?" John retorted. He was sitting on the end of Jane's desk, and she looked over at him. She liked looking at him. He was powerfully built, athletically toned, and had a face featuring a square jaw and clear blue eyes. "Good little Harley never does anything that might get him into the slightest hot water with the execs," he added. He was tossing a reader pen in the air, causing it to do precisely three flips before catching it each time. He glanced at Jane, fumbled his catch, and the pen fell to the floor.

"Hmmph. We'll see about that," Harley said. "If you're afraid to try one, then just hand 'em over. Jane will do one with me, won't you, Jane?"

"Sure. Why not," she said wearily as she laid her head back on her pillow. She let the inevitable boredom settle into her more deeply. She stared at the geodesic ceiling. Her eyes searched out the barely visible threadlike patterns of optic fibers which made up the room's dome of adjustable lighting. Bits and pieces. "Guess who I saw on my way over to class?" she asked.

"Who?" John responded.

"Bill Abrahms. That's who." With her eyes still fixed on the ceiling, Jane pulled a large quilted pillow over onto her stomach and gently clasped the soft security of it. Then suddenly she had an idea, a way to break the boredom. She sat up. "Remember him?" she said, peering over at John. "Lost it big time about a year ago. Couldn't hack it and did a deep-ender on us. The weeders had to come for him. Yeah, I saw him with a bunch of other lowlifes on my way in from shopping. It was a filthy pathetic sight—like we should feel sorry for him." She said these words, but they seemed to catch in her mouth like sticky glue as they came out, as if they didn't belong to her at all.

"Serves him right," John said snatching up another pen from her desk to toss. "He deserved weeding. He couldn't hack the money and power, and he worried too much about the lowlifes."

Jane was now deft at knowing just where in the waters to cast her line. *The final lesson made sure she knew such things.* It seemed that she had fed a lot of bait to John during the past two years, and it was now time to set the hook. His family had the kind of political juice in the conglomerates that would fit rather nicely into her current plans for the future. His dad was, in fact, head of the psychic genetics division to which she aspired to initially incorporate herself upon graduation. She was sure she had the skills to play the power-broker game. She would begin as a loyal partisan, learn what needed to be learned, and then move on. *Bits and pieces—fragments—the past divorced from the now.* Perhaps eventually, she would make a takeover strike at the likes of Data Research Inc., or maybe even Six Industries Corp. With the acquisition of either one of those, there would be no stopping her.

She was hungry to use her freshly realized skills of the lesson, and this overpowered any moral inhibitions that might still be left in her from before. The wickedness of her ambitions tingled through her and made her appetite all the more voracious for the power of the Corporates. It was time to get John to fully commit to her.

"They don't have it all that bad anyway," she said. "They're lucky we don't drive by and just blast them out of existence."

Harley laughed at this, overdoing it as usual.

"You're such a dolt Harley," John said and then aimed a wry grin at Jane.

She responded with a knowing little backward toss of her head. Every boy in the class wanted her, and she loved them wanting her. She knew how to play that game too. To make it in the conglomerates, you had to know how to play all games

"You know that term-assignment Dr. Warner gave us?" she said pretending to ignore the male jockeying for position that was going on between John and Harley. "We're supposed to figure out what should be done with the lowlifes? There are so many of them, and they have become such a nuisance—policing them and everything. I know what I'd do with them."

"What?" Harley asked eagerly.

"Did you ever want to do something for no reason other than you had the power to do it?" she asked looking directly at John.

"Yeah, I suppose so," John said uncertainly.

She noticed the slight edge of nervousness in his voice. "'Ruthlessness is never a vice in personal endeavor'—that's what Dr. Warner told me once.

"Really?" Harley said.

"Yeah, of course. This was after we hooked up in his office one day last term." She smiled and winked over at Harley, who immediately blushed to crimson. Out of the corner of her eye she could see John staring harshly at her. "I think he intends for us to hit upon that theme in our term project. As a matter of fact, I think it's critical to our final grade in his class—and it's certainly critical to success in the conglomerates."

"No problem there. I've never had any trouble with being ruthless," Harley declared.

"Shit. You're about as ruthless as a pigeon in heat," John said. "I expect you to be the next to follow in ole Abrahms footsteps." John stared coldly at Harley. Jane found this amusing.

"You think so, jockstrap?" Harley said, glaring back. "Well, listen up, because I've got an idea that might interest you, if you're not too much of a rectal wrench to be up to it. What say we take some ennui, grab a shuttle, and go out and have some fun with a few lowlifes, just for education purposes."

"What kind of fun, turd-brain?" John asked.

"Is killing a few of them fun and ruthless enough for you?"

"Could be," John responded quickly.

"I like it," Jane said. This was heading right where her bits and pieces made her want to head. Harley disgusted her; he was ugly and clumsy and was headed nowhere in corporate power politics, except for the scrap heap. In a word, he was a loser, but for now, she could use him to pry open John's weaknesses a bit, because John wasn't any too bright either.

She got up from the comfort of her lounge and went over to the window and peered down upon the campus below. The world was out there for her taking, dangling like a piece of overripe fruit. She had been training long and hard, or so she thought. The bits and pieces shoved her along. She had absorbed every important lesson, most of them written invisibly between the lines in her text books. She glanced over her shoulder at the black display cabinet that sat in the middle of her room. She eyed the white graduation box that sat on the top shelf, and felt desire for all it would bring.

She looked out the window again, and her eyes settled on the dark pond in the middle of the campus park. The promenade lights glowed brightly all around its kidney-shaped form, casting reflections of black and gold across its shimmering surface. Black and gold—she let the colors sink into her.

"Let's do it," she said suddenly. "Let's do something really awful to one of them. You know what it says on the entrance of Oliver Library— 'Might Makes Right.'"

"There are a lot of kinds of might," Harley pointed out. "Intelligent might, physical might, political might . . ."

"And you don't have any of them," John interrupted. "And what the hell do you think you know about any of it anyway?"

"I'm learning. Survival in the Mind—remember? If you weren't so busy thinking you knew it all, you might learn something too."

"Oh that's rich. Now he's full of wisdom—if only he wasn't already so full of shit and stupidity," John countered.

"I think we might find some interesting lowlifes down by the power plant," Jane interceded casually. "They like to hover around the release vents. We'll be needing a couple of blasters, though. I'm curious to see if you two are for real, or just a lot of hot air." Jane knew she was pushing all the right buttons.

And off they went, Jane in the quick lead.

They stopped in at procurement to obtain three disintegrators. John gave the duty officer a lame argument that the weapons were necessary for protection against the lowlifes, but in reaction, the officer only smiled at him and slowly shook his head no. It was against university policy to issue weapons to students, and he was not about to risk his job for some snotnosed undergraduate. At that point, Jane saw fit to mention that John's father was a good friend of the security chief for the sector, and that she understood they had been just recently discussing upcoming promotions, and that low and behold, whose name do you suppose had come up in the conversation? The officer quickly got the message. He frowned and signed out three weapons under Jane's name and I.D. card number.

What a wonderful society, she thought—barter, corruption, and manipulation, the essence of the corporates. The university had taught her well, and graduation wasn't far away. But there was another voice in her that wanted nothing of what she was feeling. *Leave it alone*, she thought.

The ennui was kicking in by now and had begun to subdue the conscience center of her brain, where all impulses of empathy, compassion, and guilt were processed and emoted, but for Jane the effect was minimal, for those emotions had already been subdued during her long years of education training, in fact during this current training session.

The three students headed toward the west end of campus where the power plant was located. It was a cold night, down in the teens, and the standard, bottom-of-the-line, student-issue commuter car was having minor circuit problems causing the vehicle to lurch slightly with un-programmed accelerations and decelerations. This was exactly the kind of thing Jane would not settle for in life after graduation—second-rate shuttles, second-rate living accommodations, second-rate lovers, second-rate anything. She was determined to have the best that life could offer, and she could find no compassion for anyone who would settle for less. The lowlifes had settled for less, hovering on the edge of existence as they did, and Jane felt they deserved whatever fate was handed down to them by those who had grabbed onto a superior station in life. All the fairness had been stacked up on her side of the tracks, and she fully intended to keep it that way.

The three students approached a group of twenty or thirty raggedly clothed vagrants who were huddled around three large steam vents located on the side of the university power plant. The building was an enormous gray structure with a single towering stack that rose above the tiny human creatures that hulked around its concrete foundation. Many of them came here to warm themselves on cold nights and to rummage through the garbage receptacles that sat at the back of the campus cafeteria across the street.

John was at the shuttle's controls, Harley sat in the back seat with his weapon holstered and peering about with excitement, and Jane had her weapon in hand ready for action.

"Let's get 'em," Harley shouted.

"No, not them," Jane said. "They're not right for our purposes . . . Ah, but look what I see over there."

She had spotted Abrahms standing with his arms folded tightly to his chest and his head bent forward to brace against the icy gusts that snapped around the corner of the power plant. She was drawn to him. Two other men and two women were standing with him in the ten foot space between vents.

Other vagrants occupied the coveted positions on either side of them in the direct path of the flow of warm, moist, vented air. John slowly maneuvered the shuttle over to the curb in front of Abrahms.

Jane opened her window halfway, and the cold night wind bit sharply into her cheeks. Occasional wafts of warm air from the nearby vents mixed in to mollify the sting of it.

Abrahms took no notice of the student's approach. His eyes were cast downward at the well-manicured grass beneath his feet, grass that managed to stay green even in early winter from the moist warmth it received from the vents. The other two men were bouncing gently up and down to keep warm. Next to Abrahms stood a woman who continually raised and lowered a hand as if to repeatedly emphasize some private and important point.

"They give me the creeps," Jane said.

John and Harley were now silent.

The other woman in the group was dressed in a dirt-laden, green, tattered, minor-exec suit. Many of its seams had frayed, and they revealed portions of her soiled undergarment. She stood at the far left end of the group and stared directly at the shuttle as it approached.

Jane pressed a button on her armrest, and her window slid all the way open. With the wind whipping into the car with full ferocity, she stuck her weapon out and aimed it at the woman.

"Just what the hell do you think you're looking at?" she called out to her.

The woman immediately lowered her eyes to the ground. This pleased Jane. The woman next to Abrahms, though, continued her repeated summoning, staring right through Jane, as if she didn't exist. Jane tried to make eye contact with her but could see that she was impervious to any powers of fear that she might wield, and so she chose to ignore her.

"Abrahms," Jane called out. "Want to go for a ride?"

Her ex-classmate did not respond, and so Jane flicked her weapon to stun and was about to fire on him, when suddenly a strange feeling swept over her. She clutched the handle of her weapon tightly, and for the flash of an instant, she found herself inside of Abrahms' dark mind of pain, looking out through eyes of despair. During that instant, her own sense of being was subdued into the background, and she winced at the sheer loneliness of Abrahms' thoughts.

A moment later the feeling passed. Must have been the ennui, she rationalized. Then she wondered whether she had experienced anything at all.

To steel herself against any further doubt or fear, she immediately raised her weapon and fired at Abrahms. The vagrants began running in all directions. Jane flicked her weapon to "kill", aimed, and fired again. An energy beam snapped out at the fleeing woman who had challenged her with a glaring look a few moments earlier, and she dropped instantly to the ground. John and Harley sat frozen in their seats, staring at the woman's scorched body as telltale wisps of smoke drifted up from her lifeless form.

The woman summoner was the only vagrant who had not budged. She had ceased her autistic repetitions, though, and now stood with her arms pinned to her sides. Her eyes blinked wildly as she pivoted her head back and forth in sharp, frightful looks. Gradually, these jerky twists of the head diminished until she was staring straight ahead again. She then began wandering slowly off in the direction of the campus exit, settling back into her repetitive summoning motion as she moved away.

Jane smiled grimly. She admired the core of brutality in her that had allowed her to so easily gun down a defenseless lowlife in cold blood. It was at that moment that she truly knew that she had the right stuff to make it in the conglomerates. That knowledge exhilarated her at first, but then it began to frighten her. She blinked away the weakness of that fear, refusing to give the slightest recognition to its roots.

"Get him into the shuttle," she yelled, pointing a finger in the direction of Abrahms' body. Her breath steamed dragon-like out into the night air.

"What about the other one?" Harley asked.

"What about her?" Jane retorted. "She's dead."

John and Harley moved over to Abrahms limp body and dragged him back to the shuttle and deposited him inside. John appeared to be shaking as he got into the driver's seat. Jane watched him with satisfaction as he sat there staring at the concrete wall of the power plant trying to re-gather his nerve. She knew he would not forget this night, and from this moment on, no matter how far he rose in the corporate ranks, he would never rise above her.

Then suddenly, before her relish could settle in, she found herself again being swept away from her own present embodiment . . . she was peering out through Abrahms' dark pallid eyes sunken inside diseased skull-bone; worthless existence pouring in; worthless life emanating out; no dignity; wild dogs had more, were more; anger swallowed up by waves of emptiness.

Then as quickly as the displacement had taken her, she was returned to her training-self. She sat dumbfounded. John and Harley had not seemed to notice, and as she began to recover, she did her best to hide it from them.

"What are you waiting for?" she asked. "Let's get him back to the dorm. You still up for a little fun?"

"Sure," Harley answered weakly.

John did not respond at all, and this now bothered Jane, for it was not like him to let Harley get the upper hand in these tug-of-wars between wills and macho. There was a part of her that was glad to see him on the verge of breaking, but it frightened her to see that such weakness was even possible, for she had seen a glimpse of it in herself. She swore she would never allow it to happen again. The training session put further demands upon her.

John drove in silence back to the dorm. He parked the vehicle out back near the loading dock. There were no campus security guards to be seen, so they dragged Abrahms to one of the two large utility elevators there. The guards certainly would not mind the students having a bit of fun with one of the lowlifes, but if they thought for an instant they were taking the vagrants in to feed them or to allow them a decent night's sleep, the guards would be sure to haul them all down to headquarters and make serious trouble for them. Jane certainly did not want to risk getting tagged with a "soft demerit," because it could be a devastating blow to her future. The many boards of directors of the conglomerates scrutinized university records very thoroughly, and they surely were not going to hire on any graduate they thought might go "bleeding-heart" on them.

John and Harley dragged Abrahms' limp body from the fifth floor elevator landing to Jane's room. As she looked on, she became giddy with the power she had already managed to gather to her, and she could not prevent a chortling laughter from leaking out. Her behavior was making John and Harley nervous, and this made her all the more giddy.

She presented her pass-key to her room's entry scanner. The latch released with a loud click, and the door slid open. As she stepped inside, another burst of laughter was on her lips, but just as it was about to sneak out of her, she was seized by a third blinding rush of displacement, and she found herself once again staring out from Abrahms' embodiment at her own greenish brown eyes.

. . . to be dead . . . nothingness . . . freedom. Life unworthy of living is death—but I want to live. I wish I didn't want to live. Scour these cold streets for the next hours for sustenance. Beg. To be free from having to take from others to nourish oneself, to

nourish with sickness. I am tired . . . so tired of hurting, of hurting others, of being hurt . . . Who warped the world so? I warped it . . . fighting, scratching, conniving, plotting, looking out only for number one, standing high on the trampled bodies. The lower I can make them, the higher I make myself. Why is it so? Who made it so? Get off by dying—but I want to live . . .

She put her hands over her face—Abrahms' face. She clawed her way out of him, refusing to be his weakness any more.

"Pathetic," she yelled out in anger. "We can't be blamed for their misery.

John and Harley looked at her skeptically.

"Get him into the room," she ordered.

John and Harley dragged Abrahms' limp body over to Jane's bed and tossed him down upon it. Jane walked directly over to the display cabinet which housed her graduation gift and opened the glass doors. She then carefully withdrew the gleaming satin-white box from the top shelf and clutched it in her hands.

"No!" John exclaimed. "You can't, Jane. You know they told us not until after graduation."

"Demolition?!" she said with a laugh. "You can't possibly believe any of that garbage. Haven't you learned anything in all your years here? There are rules, and then there are rules. The diploma is just a formality."

She opened the box impulsively and let her thoughts flow into it. She watched as the blackness inside turned into a kaleidoscope of motion and color. It changed from velvet to blue-green, then to iridescent gold, and then finally to a sunset magenta. Each nuance of each shade and tone of color spoke directly to her in a language that was specifically hers. Gradually at first, and then swiftly, she became aware of the energies that swirled around her. They had always been there, but now she could feel and read them.

Harley's thoughts bounded nervously through her mind. The fear and insecurity she had always seen in him, she could now read directly as clear emotional images. Much of his thoughts were fractured, fuzzy, misty, perforated—hollow in nature. A tiny few came into her mind solid as granite, with clear-edged boundaries that cut their message and imagery sharply into her mind. The most surprising aspect of his thoughts, though, was the slippery sheath that coated the bulk of them, a film that tried to camouflage his true nature, not only from others, but from himself. Jane pitied him for his hopeless frailty. John was right. The weeders would get him before long.

And John's thoughts were quite something to behold, too. Though some of them were solid and well-organized and registered with clarity, they were simple and one dimensional in nature. They revealed motivations similar to those that moved in Jane, but they left her feeling washed out. He had always bored her to a degree, but the dullness of his personality now rode in on every thought and became overwhelming in its pedestrian simplicity. There wasn't a creative curve or subtlety to any of it—just the hard cold purpose of survival.

Jane could not read Abrahms' thoughts in any meaningful way, nor did she dare read them for fear they might sweep her inside his depressed being again. She wished the stun would wear off him so she could do what she intended to do and be done with him. And suddenly, as if in response to this thought, Abrahms' eyes opened, and she knew immediately that indeed it was the force of her own will that had made it so. This accomplishment swept through her with its promise of further powers and momentarily took her breath away. She then willed him to sit up, and up he sat, looking at her.

"I have to tell you, Abrahms," she said. "I have a special something in store for you. You've disgraced us all. Look what you've allowed yourself to become." She laughed with hollowness.

She looked over at John and then at Harley, and they winced as she projected a devilish thought to each. The power of her dominion over them flowed like hot blood through her. She felt the bewilderment and terror that flooded into Harley's thoughts. And John's thoughts circled in a swirling frenzy of confused analysis as he tried to determine his best course of action in this situation. His predictably bland self-motivation came relentlessly in on each wave of thought-energy.

This was Jane's moment of truth. Her future depended on her ability to carry through with her intent, to do what she had the power to do. She knew that all weakness derived from the distractions of empathy, and she would not be weak. Her training session pushed her onward. *Is that what it was trying to show her?* For an instant, and only an instant, she began to worry that it wasn't.

The world within her focus became a swirl of dark energy flowing straight out of her mind, and suddenly she found herself holding each of Abrahms' molecules within the power of her will. She watched Abrahms eyes widen with horror as her telekinetic power took seize of him.

I'll show him what it's really like to be dissembled, she thought. She began to will Abrahms into an isolation far greater than she could have imagined possible before this training run.

"This is so wrong," she heard Harley thinking. "*Stop this. Please, stop this,*" he said to himself, too frightened to say it out loud, and too confused to realize that it made no difference.

Jane snapped a hateful look in his direction, and his mind retreated in terror. She returned her focus on Abrahms, and the full force of all the pent-up anguish that had been building in him suddenly broke over her like floodwaters breaking over a yielding dam. She still could not read his thoughts and emotions, but it was not necessary because once again she had been hurled back into the horrible agony that was Abrahms' being, but this time it seemed magnified a thousand-fold.

Everything in the room began to fade. The furniture, the floor, the walls, the ceiling, John, Harley—all gone. The utter aloneness that came sweeping in upon her was far worse than any separation achieved by distance, by walls, by imprisonment, even by social ostracism, for this aloneness was a complete disassociation of self from all that was "other." She was floating in a void, encapsulated in nothingness. With a shudder of deep chill, she found herself being driven further inside herself.

She screamed out. She cried. She pleaded for mercy. Each emotion plunged out into the nothingness, and each came rushing back in upon her. Her every agony became swallowed back up into the closure that was her prison of self-being, each recycled like stale breath within an air-tight helmet.

And just as her last connection to all that was outside herself was on the verge of winking out completely, a ghostly image suddenly began forming before her. It was Harley. She latched onto his form with all her powers of concentration, eating up the sight with a voracious appetite to connect back up to some aspect of life.

As the image became clearer, she stared at it, and the more she examined it, the more she realized that it was not Harley at all. It was a man with thinning gray hair and a gaunt face wrinkled severely about the eyes and mouth, age showing in every crevice. His piercing eyes burned their years of life-experience straight into her soul, and they spoke of a wisdom that was many dimensions beyond her, of an understanding and compassion that cut her like a thousand knives of truth. Her spirit wilted before him in shame.

"Professor Hammerford?" she cried out.

"Yes, that is how you know me," the image responded. "Do you know where you are?"

Jane hesitated a moment. The answer hung for an instant on the tip of her tongue, but then skittered out of reach.

"No," she said finally.

"You are in the crucible of entry. I'm sorry your schooling had to be so harsh, but after the mind wars, harsh is the only way. I can only hope that you have learned well. Do you remember why you have come here?" the old man asked, smiling at her.

She did remember something. She had been deep in meditation in her room . . . her powers had just begun to make their first rustling moves within her . . . and then she had been brought here . . . to stand before the Mind. Suddenly she realized that the University, Professor Hammerford, the conglomerates, the lowlifes, John, Harley, Abrahms, the execs—some of it, or all of it, had been built out of whole cloth in her mind. Like a thousand fragments of knowledge, it all came rocketing in upon her from the void. It was like a novel playing itself out within her, making its illusion seem real. Bits and pieces—fragments.

Tears began to bulge from her eyes. She had come here to be tested—and to enter the Mind. And she had failed miserably.

"Do you remember our warning to you about the severity of the crucible, and that it is designed to bring out the worst in a candidate?" the Professor Hammerford image asked.

She remembered, and tears began streaking down her face. What the test had brought out was far worse than anything she might have imagined. Irredeemable flaws in her character had been exposed—some real aspects of herself, primitive, subdued, exposed for her to see. Everything that had ever been important to her had been fractured into pieces, and the pieces were still dissembling themselves further, falling all around her.

She hovered in that metaphysical space, a disintegrating puff of existence, all the physicality of her human form stripped away. She was open and vulnerable. Incalculable powers circulated around her and through her. She was afraid to move, to think, to be. This was a world of thought-energy and nothing else. Think it, and it was, if it wasn't stopped by others. Matter, energy, and form existed here only as a reaction to thought, and she knew that she had no more business being here than a young child has in playing with matches.

"I can see you do yourself a great disservice," the Hammerford image said. "The base instincts of your species are given to crudeness and shortsightedness and remain dangerously un-evolved, but you must not think that the experience of your crucible lesson in any way locks you into any particular truth about yourself, or about the universe. There are many truths buried in each of us.

"It is my duty to make certain that you understand the dangers that exist within the Mind. The crucible has shaped your lesson experience to spike your negatives up, to parse out your minuses from your pluses, so that you could witness them and hopefully build an understanding from them, and I must say that you have turned out to be a most promising candidate.

"I am not worthy," Jane cried out. "I have proven that."

"On the contrary, you have demonstrated exceptional honesty and introspection in facing primitive weaknesses that we put upon you, and these in themselves are great strengths. To be sure, they are not always enough, but the Mind has granted you entry. I must remind you, though, that if you choose entry, there can be no escaping the possible consequences of that choice. Psychosis is a risk in the Mind that has taken many members. You must make a judgment as to your ability to learn to handle the powers of the Mind. If, on the other hand, you decide that you do not wish to risk the responsibilities and dangers, I will understand, and I will strip you of your powers and return you to your world.

"The power that is in you can be very intoxicating. The Mind Wars nearly destroyed us all eleven-hundred of your years ago because of that power. Necessity and survival taught us that we had to begin learning the science of the whole, and to do that we had to first learn that all 'ends' are always precisely the sum of the incremental 'means' producing them. One can never escape that reality no matter how expeditious a given action may seem at any given moment in time. The ability to see how such increments add up is what is required of any community if it is to survive. This is especially true of the community of the Mind. One does not obtain such wisdom easily, but we strongly believe that you will quickly begin learning these truths, and as a result will sustain yourself successfully in the Mind."

"I cannot risk it, not for myself, or for you in the Mind," Jane said.

The image studied her momentarily and then said, "Your respect and fear of failure is certainly to be admired. The choice before you is a difficult one, and you must weigh it carefully. Do you know why disassociation and dissemblement was such a force in your lesson?"

Jane did not.

"The ancient novel which you read when you were thirteen years old, and which you have since held in your memory as a favorite, sparks your imagination in a direction we found extremely useful. We have always admired this art your species has termed 'fiction' because it seems to empower you to travel down roads not yet travelled, to present views of your world not yet seen, and to provide tastes of the future not yet experienced. Some of the ideas contained within that favorite novel of yours have helped us form your crucible lesson for maximum learning benefit. That's why we found it useful."

"By showing me the evil in me?" Jane asked miserably, and not without some anger.

"No, that is not what it showed you. It did show you the nature of psychosis, and by showing you the exact nature of the punishment for such dementia in the Mind, a punishment, which by necessity, is far worse than the illusion of complete disembodiment and disassociation in the novel. In the Mind, you would actually be willed completely out of existence— nothing at all illusory about it—and it would have been permanent. The powers of the Mind have become so great that there can be no other way.

Jane floated in front of Hammerford and realized that other entities were present floating with her in black open space, none identifiable. They possessed energies that were highly evolved. She wanted desperately to be a part of their knowledge, their learning, their wisdom, but she feared more than anything the psychosis the Hammerford being had talked about, an ancient kernel of which, a primordial DNA bit, had been in her during her crucible lesson.

"I'm sorry, but I just can't go through with it," she said.

"There is no need for haste in your decision," Hammerford said looking at her intently. "You must be *certain*, either way."

"I think I am certain."

And with that thought, she instantly felt Hammerford's disappointment come rushing into her, followed immediately by his sorrow for having allowed such an emotion to be re-leased to her.

"As you wish, then," he said with finality.

Jane then felt the powerful hands of thought upon her, more powerful than anything she had ever before experienced. She dissolved straight away from the crucible, and as the world of the Mind vanished from her reality, she suddenly worried that she had made the wrong decision.

She peered out through her rain-streaked dorm window at the pond in the middle of the campus. The promenade lights glowed brightly around its kidney-shaped form, casting reflec-tions of gold and black across its shimmering surface.

She hated school. She hated having to learn all the inhumanity that was taught here in order to make it. She hated

John and Harley. She hated their narcissistic selfishness, and most of all she hated the apathy they wore like badges of honor, an apathy that allowed them to ignore all the suffering that went on around them. She hated their compliance with society's norms. She knew it was a self-destructive dead-end—only a matter of time.

She knew her meditations were dangerous. She had felt the power in them many times—or was it just daydreaming as others kept telling her? Counselor Simms at Business Management had warned her, "If you want to make it in the corporates, you'd better learn to stick to hard-nosed reality.

She knew the weeders were going to get her eventually anyway. If John and Harley knew what she was thinking now, the weeders would already be upon her.

She searched the blackness outside her window and felt a chill brush over her arms as the cool night air seeped in around the frame. A gold and black softness enveloped her.

And suddenly her final decision had been made, and she was gone.

"Professor Hammerford, is that you?" she called out instinctively, but no answer was returned, nor was one needed.

Ω

The Horses' Flowers

It was a cool summer day. Large pillow clouds drifted lazily overhead on a gentle breeze blowing in from Canada. The sun made an occasional peek through, turning the world from dull to bright between large shadows that crawled slowly across the landscape. It was the kind of day Kyna loved. On a day such as this things could change.

As she skipped along past Mr. Biggs' place, she saw that he was working in the small garden out behind his house next to his old barn. Kyna had always liked visiting Mr. Biggs, but she hadn't stopped by for quite some time, not since Mrs. Biggs had passed away. She had insisted that Kyna call her Marilyn, and not Mrs. Biggs.

Mr. Biggs had been fun to talk to, and kyna missed the conversations she used to have with him on Saturday mornings. She also missed Marilyn, because she would always invite Kyna in to help her bake bread, cookies, or pies. And sometimes Mr. Biggs let her give the horses treats of apples, carrots, cubes of sugar, or hay in late fall and winter. He had not been himself, though, since Mrs. Bigg's death. He stayed mostly to himself these days, and Kyna's parents discouraged her from visiting him, at least until he was ready.

The way the clouds floated by overhead probably had something to do with it, but it felt to Kyna like a good day to stop by for a visit, despite all the warnings to the contrary. And so she skipped confidently up the gravel driveway leading to the house.

"Hi, Mr. Biggs." she called out as she approached. She smiled enthusiastically, directly into the old man's leathery brown face as he looked up with a start. A cool breeze wiggled the lusty Mums growing in the corners of the garden and blew Kyna's hair gently across her mouth. "The flowers are really pretty today, aren't they?" she said.

The old man's eyes quivered momentarily with a trapped hostility that was not visible to Kyna. He blinked to shed all that he could as fast as he could.

"Where's Proxy?" Kyna asked.

"In the back pasture," Mr. Biggs said and stove his hand spade into the dark loamy earth and gouged out a weed that had begun to feel at home there. He gave the root of the weed a long, vacant look and then tossed it over onto the rotting wood pile at the end of the garden and then wiped his left eye with the back of his gray cloth glove. "That woman and her useless horses," he said at last.

"What makes you say that?" asked Kyna.

"I don't know."

"Proxy isn't useless," she protested.

Marilyn had owned three horses before her death, and had cared for them with great love. Proxy was the only horse left now. It was Kyna's favorite.

"All horses are useless, especially when they ain't put to no good use," Mr. Biggs grumbled.

"I love Proxy. He's my friend," Kyna said.

"Why are you botherin' to come around here, anyway?"

"I just thought we could talk, like we used to about things."

"About what things?"

"You know, about the weather, the horses, and Marilyn, and such things."

"Well Marilyn ain't here no more, and there's not much to be said about things you can't do nothing about, is there?"

Kyna didn't know how to respond to this and suddenly thought that mentioning Mr. Biggs' wife had been a mistake. "Uncle Charles says that Proxy is a class horse," she said trying to change the subject. "Good blood he says. I just like him because he's Proxy, though."

"Hmmmph. I oughta just sell him and be done with it," the old man grumbled in a low, nearly inaudible voice. "God knows I've got plenty of bills to pay."

"No! No! You can't sell him, Mr. Biggs!" Kyna cried out.

"Well, I should," the old man said, his voice trailing off further into some depthless place. He gouged at another weed with his spade. Harder this time. "It's a damned useless life," he mumbled. "Damned useless."

Kyna was frightened by the despair she heard in Mr. Bigg's voice. She looked down the road and thought perhaps she should leave. Her dad had told her that time would heal Mr. Biggs' sorrow, and that she should just leave him alone until it did. But a lot of time had already passed, and she could see no signs of healing. Kyna wanted Mr. Biggs to be the way he used to be. *Why did Marilyn have to die?*

Kyna stared at Mr. Biggs drawn face, and she knew it was impolite to do so. A large cloud moved in front of the sun and turned the garden dark.

"Do you miss Marilyn?" she asked.

The old man turned his spade over and banged at the soil to tamp it down. "Hell no, I don't miss her," he said. A long silence followed and then he added, "How could you miss someone like that? So impractical, that woman, even in her passing. Left me with nothin' but bills."

Kyna looked around the old ranch-style farmhouse. The yellow paint was peeling. Many of the clapboards were beginning to crack and deteriorate. Vines had taken over the south side of the house. The lawn had become a meadow of wildflowers and sprawling weeds. The many small gardens and landscaping areas that had once adorned every space around the house had now gone fallow. The juniper shrubs were scraggly and dying.

"Why do you keep up this one garden?" Kyna asked.

Mr. Biggs thrust his shovel angrily into the soil again, but did not answer.

At that moment, Kyna heard a distant ruckus of horse and human screams. The sounds were coming from quite a distance up the road. Mr. Biggs took a look in that direction, though the house completely blocked the view of the source of the commotion. But just as if he had seen clearly what was going on, his face suddenly turned into a tight knot. He threw his shovel into the dirt, ran to his pickup truck, climbed in, and drove off. With blue smoke belching from its tailpipe, the truck rattled down the long driveway, spitting up dirt and gravel behind him as it went. Just before he turned onto the road, he skidded to a sudden halt and leaned across the seat to call out to Kyna through the open window on the passenger side.

"You wait here," he yelled and then sped off again up the road.

Kyna stood still for a few moments trying to obey Mr. Bigg's wishes, but finally she gave into her fear and ran down the driveway after Mr. Biggs. When she reached the road, she began walking cautiously up its old and weathered tar surface. Horse anger and terror came to her ears mixed with a man's angry commands. When she had drawn close enough to the turmoil to see clearly, she stopped by the side of the road and watched. The sun squinted momentarily through a break in the fast moving clouds.

Mr. Biggs had already reached the commotion and had seen that Proxy had broken down a portion of the fence bordering on Mr. Kierkman's property. It was the same fence the horse had leaned against last week to reach some sprigs of alfalfa on the other side. This time Proxy had made it all the way through the fence and had been caught by Kierkman grazing on his private golf green that he had spent countless hours manicuring in a small field behind his house.

There was no doubt that the hoof prints would be difficult to putt through, Kyna thought, but Proxy didn't know any better, and Mr. Kierkman should not be yelling at him.

Kierkman was a large man, and he had thrown a rope around the horse's neck and was bending the wild-eyed animal's head down toward him, trying to pull him along toward the large colonial that was the Kierkman house.

"You let go of that animal," Mr. Biggs yelled through his open truck window as he skidded his truck to a stop.

"I'll break its fool neck, if you don't do something to keep it in your own field," Mr. Kierkman yelled back. "I warned you last time."

Kyna began running hard now as she heard the horrible anger in the yelling. She saw Mr. Biggs get out of his truck and run down a steep rocky bank toward Kierkman and the horse. "I told you to let go of that animal," he yelled. Kierkman let loose of the rope and rushed forward to meet Mr. Biggs as he reached the bottom of the bank. Proxy shook his head and mane and cried out a loud whinnie and then immediately began nibbling at the short green grass on Kierkman's golf green.

The shouting had now risen to a high pitch, and the fierceness of it frightened Kyna. Mr. Biggs shoved a finger at Kierkman's chest as he shouted something at him. Kierkman yelled something back and then shoved Mr. Biggs to the ground with great force. "Get out of here, you old fool. Everyone around here knows you're crazy these days. I'm taking custody of your horse until the authorities arrive. I don't know why you don't just put her down anyway. She's nothing but an old, broken-down nag. I've sent my wife to telephone Animal Control.

Mr. Biggs got slowly to his feet but did not look at Kierkman. He saw Kyna and looked at her only briefly, ashamedly. He muttered something and then climbed back up the bank to his truck. He tried turning around in the road and nearly backed the vehicle over the bank. His hands were shaking on the steering wheel, and he was grinding the gears on each shift into reverse and back into first. He finally managed to get enough of a turning angle to swing the truck back up the road toward his house.

A half hour later Kyna came up the drive leading Proxy by the rope that was attached to his halter. The horse towered over her and his head bobbed up and down above her blonde locks as he followed passively along. She brought him up to the front of the barn where Mr. Biggs was sitting on an old wooden cider barrel. He looked at Kyna, but his eyes were vacant and dead with defeat.

"Want me to put him in the stall?" Kyna asked.

Mr. Biggs sat staring, blinking, and working his hands over each other in a hard way.

"I'll put him away in the stall," Kyna said with insistence.

Just then a sheriff's deputy showed up in a blue and white patrol car. It was Sanders. Kierkman sat next to him in the front seat. Sanders slowly got out and explained to Mr. Biggs that Kierkman had filed for an order of impoundment for Proxy. His attorney had sited a new animal control statute, which the county had passed a few years ago. Kyna stopped and watched.

The horse bit at its halter and twisted its head as if to help the biting.

The deputy had known Mr. Biggs for many years, and when he saw the defeated look on his face he decided to let him keep the horse for the time being. Kierkman was outraged and yelled threats of legal action through the open patrol car window, but the deputy told him that such cases allow him some discretion until an official court order is issued to take the horse into county custody. He said he had decided that, for the time being at least, the horse should remain in Mr. Biggs' custody. Kierkman got out of the patrol car and advanced on Mr. Biggs.

When he arrived directly in front of him, he said, "You can bet your boots that I'll see to it that that animal of yours is taken away from you, permanently."

Mr. Biggs gave Kierkman a hard shove in the chest with both hands, and Kierkman fell back into the flower garden. As he got up, he trampled several of the Chrysanthemums growing there and made a mighty mess of the rest of the carefully tended plantings. Clumsily he gathered himself up, for Kierkman was a large clumsy man, and stepped out of the garden. He gave a quick hard look to Mr. Biggs, his lips pursed tightly, and then retreated down the driveway to the road and off to his home.

The deputy warned Mr. Biggs to keep his horse tied up, until the matter could be settled officially, and to stay away from Mr Kierkman. There was a soft tone of sympathy in his voice. He turned, got into his patrol car, and drove off. Mr. Biggs immediately stepped into the garden, being careful not to do any more damage to it than was already done from Kierkman's fall.

"Mr. Biggs, don't be sad," Kyna said. "We'll figure something out. You do love Proxy, after all, don't you?"

Mr. Biggs had begun hefting stones that had toppled from the broken stone wall, trying to put them back into place, but each time, they kept tumbling stubbornly back down to his feet. His hands were shaking.

"How can anyone love a useless animal like that?" he said in response to Kyna's assertion. He held a stone in his hand for a moment and then tossed it onto the ground as if it and the whole task, and life itself, had grown too heavy for him. Tears welled up in his eyes. A cloud darkened the sky for a moment but swiftly moved from in front of the sun. The entire house, garden, and surrounding fields glowed in golden brightness.

"The beautiful flowers in your garden aren't for people, are they?" Kyna asked.

Mr. Biggs did not respond.

"They were for the horses, weren't they? They were always for the horses. It was Marilyn's garden, and that's why she planted it, so the horses would always have something beautiful to look at in the spring and summer. And that's why you kept the garden up, isn't it, Mr. Biggs?"

Mr. Biggs looked at Kyna, and the tears began to flow freely. She moved over to him and hugged him around the waist. He hugged her back, and she could feel the desperation in the stiffness in his arms. It would be okay, though, she thought.

Ω

Novels by Terry Nearing

C-Space

The Waiting

Thought Miners

Straw Sun

Restless Waters (Penname - James Heilly)